THIS WAY TO CHRISTMAS

*It Was the Locked-out
Fairy at Last!*

THIS WAY TO CHRISTMAS

By

RUTH SAWYER

WITH ILLUSTRATIONS
IN COLORS BY
MAGINEL WRIGHT BARNEY

HARPER & BROTHERS
NEW YORK

TO DAVID

AUTHOR'S NOTE

THE author wishes to acknowledge the courtesy of Mrs. William Sharpe, who has so kindly given her permission for the adaptation of parts of Fiona Macleod's "Muime Chroisd" for the legend of St. Bridget, told here by Johanna. The author found many fragments of the legend in the north of Ireland; but nowhere was it complete as recorded by Fiona Macleod from the Island of Iona.

CONTENTS

LIST OF ILLUSTRATIONS

THIS WAY TO CHRISTMAS

I. The Chapter Before the Beginning

I WONDER if you know that stories have a way of beginning themselves? Sometimes they even do more than this. They tell themselves—beginning and ending just where they please—with no consideration at all for the author or the reader.

Perhaps you have discovered this for yourself; you may have in mind this minute some of the stories that you wished had begun long before they did—and others that ended before you thought they had any business doing so. These have a very unpleasant way of leaving your expectations and your interest all agog; and I have not a doubt that you have always blamed the author. This is not fair. In a matter of this kind an author is just as helpless as a reader, and there is no use in trying to coax or scold a story into telling itself her way. As sure as she tries the story gets sulky or hurt, picks up its beginning and ending, and trails away,

I

never to come back; and that story is lost for all time. You may try it yourself if you do not believe me.

Now, if I could have had my way, I should have begun with David in the window nook at dusk-hour, looking out on the Hill Country all white with the gathering snow; and I should have said:

"It was the year after last—and the year before next—and just seven days before Christmas—"

I have begun this way a hundred times, and every time the same thing happens. The story behaves disgracefully. It will have none of my way. I have actually heard it screaming: "No! I won't begin there! I won't—I won't—I won't!" After which it always runs for the door. As a result I have become completely cowed and I have given in. I am making believe now (and so must you, for it never does to let a story get in a bad humor) that after all this is the best beginning.

It was late fall when David's world dropped away from him; at least to David that is what seemed to happen. When one loses the very things

2

one always expects to have—big things like mother and father, home and the boys on the block—why, there is not so very much of the world left. To David, speeding toward the Hill Country on the big express with Johanna, it seemed as if there was not enough left to fill even one of the many empty days that lay before him.

It had all come about because of father being a scientist. Just what a scientist was David had never felt quite sure, but he knew it meant having a great deal of knowledge and very little time— time for boys. It also meant forgetting things that even David was supposed to remember; things like going to bed, and coming home at dinner-time, and putting on a coat when it was cold, and rubbers when it rained. Mother always laughed at these and said that father was more trouble to look after than David; and she wondered what she would do if the time ever came when she would have to decide between the two of them, and which needed her most.

And then, without any warning, that time had come. Very suddenly father came home one night

3

and announced that there was a fresh development of an almost unknown bacillus among the soldiers in the Eastern war zone; it was the chance of a lifetime for a scientist, and he would go as soon as he could pack and make necessary arrangements. The next moment he had plunged into his pocket for his note-book, and only David had seen how white and still mother had grown. When she spoke at last there was a funny little catch in her voice that sounded as if it had tried to be a laugh, but somehow could not manage it.

"I hoped and prayed that this wouldn't happen quite so soon—this having to decide between my big boy and my little boy."

Father had laughed outright. "Nonsense! There is nothing to decide. Of course you stay with David. The war country is no place for either of you, and I shall manage perfectly by myself."

"The war country is no place for David; but there are plenty of women over there working side by side with their husbands. Oh, my dear, my dear!"

Mother's arms had gathered them both in and

4

mother was holding them close. It was to father, however, that she was speaking. "I believe you are my little boy, after all. Manage! Over there! When you can't take care of yourself in your own civilized country! No, my dear, you need a mother more than David does. Besides, there's Johanna; we'll send for her. She will look after David almost as well as I can; but what would she do with you?" This time the laugh had right of way and rippled all over mother's face.

Father had stopped making notes and was looking at them both with that funny wrinkly smile about his mouth that David loved to see.

"Well, sir, what do you think about it?" he said, looking straight at David.

David had squared his shoulders and straightened his chin; but it took two hard swallows before he could answer. "I think, sir, that mother is right. You see, I'm eight, going on nine; and when a— man's that old he ought to be able to look after himself for awhile. Don't you think so?"

"He certainly ought to; but it seems that there are some who never are quite able." And father's

5

hand had suddenly reached up to mother's, which was about his shoulder.

That is all there had been to it. The next day Johanna had come—good, Irish Johanna, who had taken care of him as a baby and had stayed until he had outgrown his need of her and she had married Barney. The day after, he had said good-by to the boys on the block; and he had said it as one about to depart upon a rare adventure, taking his leave of less fortunate comrades. He did not intend that they should discover how much of his world had dropped away from him, or how he envied them the continued possession of theirs. Moreover, it increased his courage threefold to make believe that what had happened was not so bad, after all. In this manner he was able to assume an added stature, one fitting his newly acquired manhood, when the time came to swing the door of his home tight shut and he was able to say a brave good-by to father and mother.

Now it was all over. He and Johanna were speeding toward the Hill Country, and he was glad, very glad, to be a little boy again and snuggle into

6

the hollow of Johanna's arm as he had been used to doing in the old nursery days. After all, eight-going-on-nine is not so very old.

David wasted no time. Out of the scraps that were left him he tried at once to build up a new world. He looked out of the car window at the fields and houses flying past, and he thought of all the pleasant things Johanna had promised him. Johanna and Barney were the caretakers of a big summer hotel in the mountains. The summer season was over, the hotel closed, and he was going to live with Johanna and Barney in the lodge and have a whole mountain-top to play on. He was going to help Barney cut down next year's fire-wood and drive the sledge for him over the lumber roads. He was going to make a toboggan slide down the cleared side of the mountain; he was going to skate on the pond above the beaver dam, and learn to skee, and a crowd of other jolly things. And in the spring there were to be the maple-trees to tap. Only, in the meantime, there were father and mother traveling farther and farther away; and there was Christmas coming nearer and nearer.

7

And how could he ever stand one without the others?

He turned away from the car window and looked at Johanna; and then out popped the most surprising question from her.

"Hark, laddy! Have ye forgotten all about the fairies and the stories Johanna used to tell?"

David smiled without knowing it.

"Why, no. No, I haven't. A person never entirely forgets about fairies, even if he does grow up —does he? I guess I haven't been thinking about them lately, that's all."

"Sure, and ye haven't!" Johanna's voice had the same folksy ring to it that it had had in the nursery days. "Faith, 'tis hard keeping them lively when ye are living in the city. Wasn't I almost giving over believing in them myself, after living there a few years? It wasn't till I moved to the hilltops and the green country that I got them back again."

"Have you seen any up there?"

David asked it as one might inquire about the personal habits of Santa Claus or the chances of finding the crock of gold at the rainbow's end, experi-

8

ences one has never had oneself, but which one is perfectly willing to credit to another upon receipt of satisfactory evidence. Moreover, fairies were undeniably comfortable to think about just now. And what is more, whenever things happen that seem unreal and that make you feel strange and unreal yourself, that is the very time that fairies become the most real and easy to believe in. David discovered this now, and it made him snuggle closer to Johanna and repeat his question:

"Have you really seen any up there?"

Johanna puckered her forehead and considered for a moment.

" 'Tis this way, laddy. I can't be saying honestly that I have laid my two eyes on one for certain; and then again I can't say honestly that I haven't. Many's the time in the woods or thereabouts that I've had the feeling I've just stumbled on one, just missed him by a wink, or beaten him there by a second. The moss by the brookside would have a trodden-down look and the bracken would be swaying with no help o' the wind—for all the world as if a wee man had just been brushing his way through."

9

"It might have been a squirrel," suggested David, the dust of the city still clouding his mind.

"Aye, but I'm thinking it wasn't. And if there's a fairy up yonder in the Hill Country, I'm thinking ye'll find him. 'Twill give ye one thing more to do, eh, laddy?" Johanna tightened the arm about him and laughed softly.

"But how would fairies get over here? I shouldn't think they would ever want to leave Ireland; and I thought they never came out in winter."

"They might come because they had been locked out." Johanna's eyes suddenly began to dance mysteriously, and she put her lips close to David's ear that the noise and jar of the train might not drown one word of what she was going to say:

"Whist, laddy! Do ye mind what day it is? 'Tis the very last day of the fairy summer, the last day when they'll be making the rings and dancing the reels over in Ireland."

"Why, it's Hallowe'en!" remembered David.

"Aye, that's what! And after this night the fairies bolt the doors of their raths fast with magic and never come out again till May Eve, barring once

It Happens Every So Often That a Fairy Gets Locked Out

in a white winter or so when they come out on Christmas Eve. But it happens every so often that a fairy gets locked out on this night. He stays dancing too long, or playing too many tricks, and when he gets back to the rath 'tis past cock-crow and the door is barred against him. Then there's naught for him to do but to bide how and where he can till opening time comes on May Eve."

"And if—and if—"

"Sure, if one should get locked out this night, what's to prevent his coming over? What's more likely than that he'd be saying to himself, 'Faith, Ireland 'll be a mortal lonely place with the rest o' the lads gone. I'll try my luck in another country.' And with that he follows the rest of the Irish and emigrates over here. And if he ever lands, ye mark my word, laddy, he'll make straight for the Hill Country! That is, if he's not there already ahead of himself."

Johanna laughed and David laughed with her.

"Sure, there's a heap o' sense in some nonsense, mind that! And never be so foolish, just because ye grow up and get a little book knowledge, as to turn

11

up your nose and mock at the things ye loved and believed in when ye were a little lad. Them that do, lose one of the biggest cures for heartache there is in the world, mind that!"

David turned back to the window. Already, beyond the foreground of passing woods and meadows, he could catch glimpses of the Hill Country, hazy and purple, lying afar off. Johanna was right. It was better to think of the locked-out fairy than of himself. He found himself wondering if fairies grew lonesome as humans did, and if it was as hard to be locked out of a rath as a home. He wondered if all the fairies were grown up or if there were boy and girl fairies, and father and mother fairies. He would ask Johanna sometime, when he was sure he could ask it with a perfectly steady voice. But most of all, he wondered about opening time; and he wished with all his heart that he knew just when opening time would come for him. Until then he must keep very busy with the fire-wood and the sled and the toboggan-slide and the skating and skeeing and Christmas.

What kind of a Christmas was it going to be?

12

The train climbed half-way to the top of the highest hill and there it left David and Johanna. Barney was waiting for them with the horses and the big wagon to carry them up the rest of the way; and to David it seemed a very lonesome way. The stars were out before they reached the lodge, but even in the starlight he could see that they were alone on the hilltop except for the great, shadowy, closed hotel and the encompassing fir-trees.

"Ye'll not be troubled with noise, and ye'll not be pestered with neighbors," laughed Barney, as he helped David to clamber down from the wagon. "Johanna says that in the winter there is nobody alive in these parts but the creatures and the 'heathens' and ourselves."

II. The Locked-out Fairy

TWO months had passed since David had come to the Hill Country—two months in which he had thrown himself with all the stoutness of heart he could muster into the new life and the things Johanna had promised. He had spent long, crisp November days with Barney in the woods, watching him fell the trees marked for firewood and learning to use his end of a cross-cut saw. When the snow came and the lumber roads were packed hard for sledding he had shared in the driving of the team and the piling of the logs. He had learned to skee and to snow-shoe; already he had dulled his skates on the pond above the beaver dam. Yet in spite of all these things, in spite of Barney's good-natured comradeship and Johanna's faithful care and love, the ache in his heart had grown deeper until his loneliness seemed to shut him in like the snow-capped hills about him. And now it was seven days before Christmas—and not a word had been said concerning it.

14

David had begun to wonder if in all that country of bare hilltops and empty valleys, of snow and fir-tree and wild creature, there was anything out of which one could possibly make a Christmas. And slowly the conviction had been borne in upon him that there was not. The very thought of the toy-stores in the city, of the windows with their displays of Christmas knickknacks, of the street booths covered with greens, of what the boys on the block were doing and talking about, of the memories of all the other Christmases that had been, brought unspeakable pangs to his soul. He wondered how he was ever going to stand it—this Christmas that was no Christmas.

And this is how it happened that at dusk-hour, seven days before Christmas, a very low-spirited boy of eight-going-on-nine sat curled up on the window-seat of the lodge, looking out through the diamond panes and wishing with all his heart that he was somebody else in some other place and that it was some other time of the year.

Barney was always bedding down the horses at this time and Johanna was getting supper; and as there was never anything in particular for David to do it had become a custom with him to watch for the lighting of the lamps in the cabins of the "heathen." There were four cabins—only one was a cottage; and he could see them all from the lodge by a mere change of position or window. Somehow he liked them, or thought he should like them if he knew them, in spite of all the unalluring things Johanna had said about them. According to her the families who lived in them were outcasts, speaking strange tongues and worshiping strange gods, and quite unfit to cross the door-steps of honest Christian folk. David hardly knew whether Barney shared this opinion or not. Barney teased Johanna a good deal and laughed at her remarks every time she aired her grievance: that there should be no decent neighbors like themselves on all that barren hilltop. In his own heart David clung persistently to the feeling that he should like them all if he ever got near enough to make their acquaintance.

It was always the "lunger's" lamp that shone out first in the dusk. David could usually tell to the minute when it would be lighted by watching the shadow on the foot-hill. Johanna was uncertain from what country these neighbors had come, but she thought it was Portugal. And Portuguese! Words always failed her when she tried to convey to David the exact place that Portuguese held among the heathen; but he was under the impression that it must be very near the top. One of these neighbors was sick with bad lungs, so his family had come to try the open-air cure of the hills; and they had been here since early spring. David never saw their tiny spark of light spring out against the dark of the gathering gloom that he did not make a wish that the "lunger" might be a good deal better the next day.

Across the ridge from the foot-hill lay the lumber camp, and here David always looked for the second light. The camp was temporarily deserted, the company having decided to wait a year or two before cutting down any more timber, and the loggers had been sent to another camp farther north. Only the cook, an old negro, had remained behind to guard the property from fire and poachers, and he it was that lighted in his shack the solitary lamp that sent its twinkling greeting up to David every night.

17

Straight down the hill shone the third light, from the trapper's cabin, and it was always close to dark before that was lighted. What the trapper's nationality was Johanna had never happened to specify; but she had often declared that he was one of those bad-looking dark men from the East—Asia, perhaps; and she had not a doubt that he had come to the woods to escape the law. David's mental picture of him was something quite dreadful; and yet when his light sprang out of the dark and twinkled at him up the white slope he always found himself desperately sorry for the trapper, alone by himself with the creatures he had trapped or shot—and his thoughts.

The fourth light came through another window, shining up from the opposite slope of the hill—the slope that led toward the station and the village beyond. This was the flagman's light and it hung in the little hut by the junction where the main railroad crossed the circuit line. It was always lighted when David looked for it, and he always sat watching until he should see the colored signal-lights swing out on the track beyond, for then he knew the flagman's work was over for the day—that is, if all was well on the road. It happened sometimes, however, that there was a snow-slide down the ravine above the crossing, or sometimes a storm uprooted a tree and hurled it across the track, and then the flagman was on guard all night. Now, the flagman was German; and Johanna's voice always took on a particularly forbidding and contemptuous tone whenever she spoke of him. David had often marveled at this, for in the city his father had friends who were German and they were very good friends. Once David had spoken his mind:

"I don't see why you call him a heathen, Johanna, just because he was born in the country that's making the war. It wasn't his fault—and I don't see why that's any reason for treating him as if he had made the trouble himself."

"Well, how do ye think we'd be treated if we were over there now in that heathen's country? Sure, ye wouldn't find them loving us any to speak of." Johanna's lips had curled scornfully. "Ye can take my word for it, laddy, if we were there the same as he's here we would be counting ourselves lucky to be alive at all, and not expecting to be asked in for any tea-drinking parties."

It troubled David, none the less, this strange unfriendliness of Johanna's; and this night the weight of it hung particularly heavy upon him. He turned back to his window nook with a heart made heavier by this condition of alienage. No family, no neighbors, no Christmas—it was a dreary outlook; and he could not picture a single face or a single hearthside behind those four lights that blinked at him in such a friendly fashion.

He realized suddenly that he was very tired. Half the day he had spent clearing a space on the beaver pond big enough for skating; and clearing off a day's fall of snow with a shovel and a broom is hard work. He leaned against the window niche and pillowed his head on his arm. He guessed he would go to bed right after supper. Wouldn't it be fun now, if he could wish himself into one of those cabins, whichever one he chose, and see what was happening there this minute? If he had found the locked-out fairy Johanna had talked so much about he might have learned wishing magic from him.

20

What had happened to the fairy, anyway? Of course it was half a tale and half a joke; nevertheless the locked-out fairy had continued to seem very real to him through these two months of isolation, and wherever he had gone his eye had been always alert for some sign of him. Unbelievable as it may seem, the failure to find him had brought keen disappointment. David had speculated many times as to where he might be living, where he would find his food, how he would keep himself warm. A fairy's clothes were very light, according to Johanna. Undoubtedly he had come over in just his green jerkin and knee-breeches, with stockings and slippers to match; and these were not fit covering for winter weather like this.

David smiled through half-shut eyes. The fairy might steal a pelt from the trapper's supply; that would certainly keep him warm; and if he were anything of a tailor he could make himself a cap and a coat in no time. Or, better yet, he might pick out one that just fitted him and creep into it without having to make it over; a mink's skin would be about the right size, or a squirrel's. His smile deepened at

21

his own conceit. Then something in the dusk outside caught his eye. Some small creature was hopping across the snow toward the lodge.

David flattened his nose to the window to see better, and made out very distinctly the pointed ears, curved back, and long, bushy tail of a squirrel—a gray squirrel. At once he thought of some nuts in his jacket pocket, nuts left over from an after-dinner cracking. He dug for them successfully, and opening the window a little he dropped them out. Nearer came the squirrel, fearlessly eager, oblivious of the eyes that were watching him with growing interest. He reached the nuts and was nosing them about for the most appetizing when he sat up suddenly on his hind legs, clutching the nut of his choice between his fore paws and cocking his head as he did so toward the window.

The effect on David was magical. He gave his eyes one insistent rub and then opened the window wider.

"Come in," he called, softly. "Please do come in!"

For he had seen under the alert little ears some-

thing quite different from the sharp nose and whisk-
ers of the every-day squirrel. There were a pair of
blue eyes that winked outrageously at him, while a
round, smooth face wrinkled into smiles and a
mouth knowingly grinned at him. It was the locked-
out fairy at last!

He bobbed his head at David's invitation, fastened
his little white teeth firmly in the nut, and scrambled
up the bush that grew just outside. A minute more
and he was through the window and down beside
David on the seat.

"Ah—ee, laddy, where have your eyes been this
fortnight?" he asked. "I've whisked about ye and
chattered down at ye from half a score o' pine-trees
—and ye never saw me!"

David colored shamefully.

"Never mind. 'Tis a compliment ye've been paying to my art," and the fairy cocked his head and
whisked his tail and hopped about in the most con-
vincing fashion.

David held his sides and rocked back and forth
with merriment. "It's perfect," he laughed; "simply perfect!"

"Aye, 'tis fair; but I've not mastered the knack o' the tail yet. I can swing it grand, but I can't curl it up stylish. I can fool the mortals easy enough, but ye should see the looks the squirrels give me sometimes when I'm after trying to show off before them."

There was nothing but admiration in David's look of response. "The coat fits you splendidly," he said.

"Sure—'tis as snug as if it grew on me. But I miss my pockets, and I'm not liking the color as well as if it were green."

David laughed again. "Why, I believe you are as Irish as Johanna!"

"And why shouldn't I be? Faith, there are worse faults, I'm thinking. Now tell me, laddy, what's ailing ye? Ye've been more than uncommon downhearted lately."

"How did you know?"

"Could a wee fairy man be watching ye for a fortnight, coming and going, and not know?"

"Well, it's lonesomeness; lonesomeness and Christmas." David owned up to it bravely.

24

" 'Tis easy guessing ye're lonesome—that's an ailment that's growing chronic on this hillside. But what's the matter with Christmas?"

"There isn't any. There isn't going to be any Christmas!" And having at last given utterance to his state of mind, David finished with a sorrowful wail.

"And why isn't there, then? Tell me that."

"You can't make Christmas out of miles of snow and acres of fir-trees. What's a boy going to do when there aren't any stores or things to buy, or Christmas fixings, or people, and nobody goes about with secrets or surprises?"

The fairy pushed back the top of his head and the gray ears fell off like a fur hood, showing the fairy's own tow head beneath. He reached for his thinking-lock and pulled it vigorously.

"I should say," he said at last, "that a boy could do comfortably without them. Sure, weren't there Christmases long before there were toy-shops? No, no, laddy. Christmas lies in the hearts and memories of good folk, and ye'll find it wherever ye can find them!"

25

David shook his head doubtfully.

"I don't see how that can be; but even suppose it's true, there aren't even good folk here."

The fairy grinned derisively and wagged his furry paw in the direction of the lights shining on the hill-side:

"What's the meaning of that, and that, and that? Now I should be calling them good folk, the same as ye here."

"Hush!" David looked furtively toward the door that led into the kitchen. "It wouldn't do to let Johanna hear you. Why, she thinks—"

The fairy raised a silencing paw to his lips.

"Whist, there, laddy! If ye are after wanting to find Christmas ye'd best begin by passing on naught but kind sayings. Maybe ye are not knowing it, but they are the very cairn that mark the way to Christmas. Now I'll drive a bargain with ye. If ye'll start out and look for Christmas I'll agree to help ye find the road to it."

"Yes," agreed David, eagerly.

"But there's one thing ye must promise me. To put out of your mind for all time these notions that ye are bound to find Christmas hanging with the tinsel balls to the Christmas tree or tied to the end of a stocking. Ye must make up your mind to find it with your heart and not with your fingers and your eyes."

"But," objected David, "how can you have Christmas without Christmas things?"

"Ye can't. But ye've got the wrong idea entirely about the things. Ye say now that it's turkey and plum-cake and the presents ye give and the presents ye get; and I say 'tis thinkings and feelings and sayings and rememberings. I'm not meaning, mind ye, that there is anything the matter with the first lot, and there's many a fine Christmas that has them in, but they'll never make a Christmas of themselves, not in a thousand years. And what's more, ye can do grand without them."

David rubbed his forehead in abject bewilderment. It was all very hard to understand; and as far as he could see the fairy was pointing out a day that sounded like any ordinary day of the year and not at all like Christmas. But, thanks to Johanna, David had an absolute faith in the infallibility of

27

fairies. If he said so it must be true; at least it was worth trying. So he held out his hand and the fairy laid a furry paw over the ball of his forefinger in solemn compact.

"It's a bargain," David said.

"It is that," agreed the fairy. "And there's nothing now to hinder my going."

He pulled the gray ears over his tow head again until there was only a small part of fairy left.

"Don't ye be forgetting," he reminded David as he slipped through the window. "I'll be on the watch out for ye the morrow."

David watched him scramble down the bush, stopping a moment at the bottom to gather up the remainder of the nuts, which he stuffed away miraculously somewhere between his cheek and the fur. Then he raised a furry paw to his ear in a silent salute.

"Good-by," said David, softly, "good-by. I'm so glad you came."

And it seemed to him that he heard from over the snow the fairy's good-by in Gaelic, just as Barney or Johanna might have said it: *"Beanacht leat!"*

28

III. Barney's Tale of the Wee Red Cap

DAVID watched the locked-out fairy go forth into the dusk again. He had always supposed that fairies disappeared suddenly and mysteriously; but this was not so. The little gray furry figure hopped slowly across the patch of white in front of the window, bobbed and frisked, pricked up the alert little ears, and swung his bushy tail, after the fashion of any genuine squirrel, and then dove under the low-hanging boughs of the nearest evergreens. As he disappeared, David felt an arm on his shoulder and turned to blink wonderingly into the face of big Barney bending over him and grinning.

"Well, well, who'd have thought to catch the sandman making his rounds afore supper! What sent ye to sleep, laddy?"

"Asleep!" David scoffed hotly at the accusation. "I was no more asleep than you are, Barney. Why, do you know what I've seen, what's been right here this very minute?"

Barney's grin broadened. "Well, maybe now it was the locked-out fairy!" For this was the old joke between them.

Little did Barney dream that this time he had not only touched upon the real truth, but he had actually gripped it by the scruff of the neck, as he would have put it himself. David looked wise. He was trying to make up his mind just how best to tell the wonderful news when Barney's next words held his tongue and sent the news scuttling back to his memory.

"And speaking o' fairies, I was just asking Johanna—getting supper out yonder—did she mind the tale Old Con, the tinker, used to be telling back in the Old Country about his great-uncle Teig and the wee red cap. Did Johanna ever tell ye, now, about the fairies' red cap?"

David shook his head.

"It serves as an easy way o' travel for them; ye might almost call it their private Pullman car," Barney chuckled. "Ye wait a minute and I'll see is

30

there time to tell the tale myself atween now and supper."

He was away to the kitchen and back before David had much more than time enough to rub the gathering frost from the window-pane and look out for a possible return of his fairy. Nothing was to be seen, however, but the snow and the trees and the trail of tiny footprints; and big Barney was beside him in the window nook again, with a mysterious "knowledgeable look" on his face.

"Aye, there's time and light enough still in the west to see the tale through." He paused for an instant.

"Ye know, laddy, over in Ireland they're not keeping Christmas the same as ye do here—the poor, I mean. 'Tis generally the day after, St. Stephen's Day, tho' sometimes 'tis St. Stephen's Eve that they manage a bit of a feast and merrymaking. Them that has little shares with them that has less; and afterward the neighbors gather about the turf fire for a story-telling. Aye, many's the strange tale ye will hear over in Ireland on one of them nights. And here's the tale Old Con, the tinker, used for

31

to be telling about his great-uncle Teig—the most close-fisted man in all of Inneskillen."

And here again is the tale as Barney retold it and David heard it, as he sat in the window nook of the lodge at dusk-hour just seven days before Christmas.

It was the Eve of St. Stephen, and Teig sat alone by his fire with naught in his cupboard but a pinch of tea and a bare mixing of meal, and a heart inside of him as soft and warm as the ice on the water-bucket outside the door. The turf was near burnt on the hearth—a handful of golden cinders left, just; and Teig took to counting them greedily on his fingers.

"There's one, two, three, an' four an' five," he laughed. "Faith, there be more bits o' real gold hid undther the loose clay in the corner."

It was the truth; and it was the scraping and scrooching for the last piece that had left Teig's cupboard bare of a Christmas dinner.

"Gold is betther nor eatin' an' dthrinkin'. An' if ye have naught to give, there'll be naught asked of ye." And he laughed again.

32

He was thinking of the neighbors, and the doles of food and piggins of milk that would pass over their thresholds that night to the vagabonds and paupers who were sure to come begging. And on the heels of that thought followed another: who would be giving old Shawn his dinner? Shawn lived a stone's throw from Teig, alone, in a wee tumbled-in cabin; and for a score of years past Teig had stood on the door-step every Christmas Eve, and, making a hollow of his two hands, had called across the road:

"Hey, there, Shawn, will ye come over for a sup?"

And Shawn had reached for his crutches, there being but one leg to him, and had come.

"Faith," said Teig, trying another laugh, "Shawn can fast for the once; 'twill be all the same in a month's time." And he fell to thinking of the gold again.

A knock came to the door. Teig pulled himself down in his chair where the shadow would cover him, and held his tongue.

"Teig, Teig!" It was the Widow O'Donnelly's

voice. "If ye are there, open your door. I have not got the pay for the spriggin' this month, an' the childther are needin' food."

But Teig put the leash on his tongue, and never stirred till he heard the tramp of her feet going on to the next cabin. Then he saw to it that the door was tight barred. Another knock came, and it was a stranger's voice this time:

"The other cabins are filled; not one but has its hearth crowded. Will ye take us in, the two of us? The wind bites mortal sharp; not a morsel o' food have we tasted this day. Masther, will ye take us in?"

But Teig sat on, a-holding his tongue; and the tramp of the strangers' feet passed down the road. Others took their place—small feet, running. It was the miller's wee Cassie, and she called out as she went by:

"Old Shawn's watchin' for ye. Ye'll not be forgettin' him, will ye, Teig?"

And then the child broke into a song, sweet and clear, as she passed down the road:

34

"Listen all ye, 'tis the Feast o' St. Stephen,
  Mind that ye keep it, this holy even.
  Open your door and greet ye the stranger,
  For ye mind that the wee Lord had naught but a manger.
                                    Mhuire as truagh!

"Feed ye the hungry and rest ye the weary,
  This ye must do for the sake of Our Mary.
  'Tis well that ye mind—ye who sit by the fire—
  That the Lord He was born in a dark and cold byre.
                                    Mhuire as truagh!"

Teig put his fingers deep in his ears. "A million murdthering curses on them that won't let me be! Can't a man try to keep what is his without bein' pesthered by them that has only idled and wasted their days?"

And then the strange thing happened: hundreds and hundreds of wee lights began dancing outside the window, making the room bright; the hands of the clock began chasing each other round the dial, and the bolt of the door drew itself out. Slowly, without a creak or a cringe, the door opened, and in there trooped a crowd of the Good People. Their wee green cloaks were folded close about them, and each carried a rush-candle.

35

Teig was filled with a great wonderment, entirely, when he saw the fairies, but when they saw him they laughed.

"We are takin' the loan o' your cabin this night, Teig," said they. "Ye are the only man hereabouts with an empty hearth, an' we're needin' one."

Without saying more, they bustled about the room making ready. They lengthened out the table and spread and set it; more of the Good People trooped in, bringing stools and food and drink. The pipers came last, and they sat themselves around the chimney piece a-blowing their chanters and trying the drones. The feasting began and the pipers played, and never had Teig seen such a sight in his life. Suddenly a wee man sang out:

"Clip, clap, clip, clap, I wish I had my wee red cap!"

And out of the air there tumbled the neatest cap Teig had ever laid his two eyes on. The wee man clapped it on his head, crying:

"I wish I was in Spain!" And—whist!—up the chimney he went, and away out of sight!

It happened just as I am telling it. Another wee

36

*Slowly the Door Opened, and
in There Trooped a Crowd
of the Good People*

man called for his cap, and away he went after the first. And then another and another until the room was empty and Teig sat alone again.

"By my soul," said Teig, "I'd like to thravel like that myself! It's a grand savin' of tickets an' baggage; an' ye get to a place before ye've had time to change your mind. Faith, there is no harm done if I thry it."

So he sang the fairies' rhyme and out of the air dropped a wee cap for him. For a moment the wonder had him, but the next he was clapping the cap on his head, crying:

"Spain!"

Then—whist!—up the chimney he went after the fairies, and before he had time to let out his breath he was standing in the middle of Spain, and strangeness all about him.

He was in a great city. The doorways of the houses were hung with flowers and the air was warm and sweet with the smell of them. Torches burned along the streets, sweetmeat-sellers went about crying their wares, and on the steps of a cathedral crouched a crowd of beggars.

37

"What's the meanin' o' that?" asked Teig of one of the fairies.

"They are waiting for those that are hearing Mass. When they come out they give half of what they have to those that have nothing, so that on this night of all the year there shall be no hunger and no cold."

And then far down the street came the sound of a child's voice, singing:

"Listen all ye, 'tis the Feast o' St. Stephen,
Mind that ye keep it, this holy even."

"Curse it!" said Teig. "Can a song fly afther ye?" And then he heard the fairies cry, "Holland!" and he cried, "Holland!" too.

In one leap he was over France, and another over Belgium, and with the third he was standing by long ditches of water frozen fast, and over them glided hundreds upon hundreds of lads and maids. Outside each door stood a wee wooden shoe, empty. Teig saw scores of them as he looked down the ditch of a street.

"What is the meanin' o' those shoes?" he asked the fairies.

38

"Ye poor lad!" answered the wee man next to him. "Are ye not knowing anything? This is the Gift Night of the year, when every man gives to his neighbor."

A child came to the window of one of the houses, and in her hand was a lighted candle. She was singing as she put the light down to close the glass, and Teig caught the words:

"Open your door and greet ye the stranger,
For ye mind that the wee Lord had naught but a manger.
Mhuire as truagh!"

" 'Tis the de'il's work!" cried Teig, and he set the red cap more firmly on his head. "I'm for another country."

I cannot be telling you half of the adventures Teig had that night, nor half the sights that he saw. But he passed by fields that held sheaves of grain for the birds, and door-steps that held bowls of porridge for the wee creatures. He saw lighted trees, sparkling and heavy with gifts; and he stood outside the churches and watched the crowds pass in, bearing gifts to the Holy Mother and Child.

39

At last the fairies straightened their caps and cried, "Now for the great hall in the King of England's palace!"

Whist—and away they went, and Teig after them; and the first thing he knew he was in London, not an arm's-length from the King's throne. It was a grander sight than he had seen in any other country. The hall was filled entirely with lords and ladies; and the great doors were open for the poor and the homeless to come in and warm themselves by the King's fire and feast from the King's table. And many a hungry soul did the King serve with his own hands.

Those that had anything to give gave it in return. It might be a bit of music played on a harp or a pipe, or it might be a dance or a song; but more often it was a wish, just, for good luck and safe-keeping.

Teig was so taken up with the watching that he never heard the fairies when they wished themselves off; moreover, he never saw the wee girl that was fed and went laughing away. But he heard a bit of her song as she passed through the door:

40

"Feed ye the hungry and rest ye the weary,
   This ye must do for the sake of Our Mary."

Then the anger had Teig. "I'll stop your pestherin' tongue once an' for all time!" And, catching the cap from his head, he threw it after her.

No sooner was the cap gone than every soul in the hall saw him. The next moment they were about him, catching at his coat and crying:

"Where is he from? What does he here? Bring him before the King!"

And Teig was dragged along by a hundred hands to the throne where the King sat.

"He was stealing food," cried one.

"He was stealing the King's jewels," cried another.

"He looks evil," cried a third. "Kill him!"

And in a moment all the voices took it up and the hall rang with, "Aye, kill him, kill him!"

Teig's legs took to trembling, and fear put the leash on his tongue; but after a long silence he managed to whisper:

"I have done evil to no one, no one!"

"Maybe," said the King. "But have ye done good?

41

Come, tell us, have ye given aught to anyone this night? If ye have, we will pardon ye."

Not a word could Teig say; fear tightened the leash, for he was knowing full well there was no good to him that night.

"Then ye must die," said the King. "Will ye try hanging or beheading?"

"Hanging, please, your Majesty," said Teig.

The guards came rushing up and carried him off. But as he was crossing the threshold of the hall a thought sprang at him and held him.

"Your Majesty," he called after him, "will ye grant me a last request?"

"I will," said the King.

"Thank ye. There's a wee red cap that I'm mortal fond of, and I lost it awhile ago; if I could be hung with it on I would hang a deal more comfortable."

The cap was found and brought to Teig.

"Clip, clap, clip, clap, for my wee red cap. I wish I was home!" he sang.

Up and over the heads of the dumfounded guard he flew, and—whist!—and away out of sight. When he opened his eyes again he was sitting close by his own hearth, with the fire burnt low. The hands of the clock were still, the bolt was fixed firm in the door. The fairies' lights were gone, and the only bright thing was the candle burning in old Shawn's cabin across the road.

A running of feet sounded outside, and then the snatch of a song:

" 'Tis well that ye mind, ye who sit by the fire,
That the Lord He was born in a dark and cold byre.
Mhuire as truagh!"

"Wait ye, whoever ye are!" And Teig was away to the corner, digging fast at the loose clay, as the terrier digs at a bone. He filled his hands full of the shining gold, then hurried to the door, unbarring it.

The miller's wee Cassie stood there, peering at him out of the darkness.

"Take those to the Widow O'Donnelly, do ye hear? And take the rest to the store. Ye tell Jamie to bring up all that he has that is eatable an' dhrinkable; an' to the neighbors ye say, 'Teig's keepin' the feast this night.' Hurry now!"

Teig stopped a moment on the threshold until the tramp of her feet had died away; then he made a hollow of his two hands and called across the road:

"Hey, there, Shawn, will ye come over for a sup?"

"And hey, there, the two o' ye, will ye come out for a sup?"

It was Johanna's cheery voice bringing David back from a strange country and stranger happenings. She stood in the open doorway, a lighted candle in her hand.

"Ye'd hurry faster if ye knew what I had outside for supper. What would a wee lad say, now, to a bit o' real Irish currant-bread, baked in the griddle, and a bowl of chicken broth with dumplings!"

IV. David Goes Seeking the Way to Christmas and Finds the Flagman

ALL night long the snow fell, and when David wakened the hilltop was whiter than ever, if such a thing could be. The tiny prints in the snow that had marked the trail of the locked-out fairy were gone.

For a moment David wondered if he could have dreamed it all, and then he knew it could not be just a dream. It must be something more, to bring such good Christmas news—news that lasted all through the night and wakened him with a song in his heart and a gladness that a new day had come. And what a day it was! An orange sun was breaking the gray of the dawn; he could hear the soft push and pound of Barney's shovel clearing a pathway from the door to the road, and he knew he could be off early on his skees, down the hill to—where he did not know. But

45

the fairy had promised that if he should start out seeking the way to Christmas he would help him.

He dressed quickly to the swinging rhythm of the reel Johanna was lilting in the kitchen below; for in a little lodge bedroom on a hilltop, with the thermometer outside many degrees below zero, one does not dally in putting on one's clothes. He came down to breakfast for the first time since he had left the old home without having to pretend anything in the way of feelings; and he found beside his plate a letter from father.

"Barney, the rascal, brought it back with him yesterday and carried it about in his pocket all evening, never thinking of it once," Johanna explained, shaking her fist at that guilty person just coming in.

"Sure, the two of us were that busy entertaining fairies last night we hadn't mind enough for anything else." And Barney winked at David knowingly.

David responded absent-mindedly. His thoughts and fingers were too busy with the letter to pay much attention to anything else. Father had little time for boys, as we have already said, but when he did take

46

time the results were unquestionably satisfactory; the letter proved this. It was a wonderful letter, full of all the most interesting seeings and doings—just the things a boy loves to hear about—and yet it was written as any grown-up would write to another. That was one fine thing about father. When he did have time for boys he never looked down upon them as small people with little wisdom and less understanding; he always treated them as equals. But it was what came at the very last of the letter that brought the joyful smile to David's lips.

Johanna and Barney saw it and smiled to each other.

"Good news, laddy?" Johanna asked.

"There's nothing about coming home, but there's something about Christmas." David consulted the letter again. "Father says he's been looking around for some time for just the right present to send for Christmas, and he's just found it. He thinks I'll like it about the best of anything, and it ought to get here —unless the steamers are awfully delayed—on Christmas day."

"That's grand!" Barney beamed his own delight

47

over the news. "What do ye think it might be, now?"

David shook his head.

"I don't know—don't believe I could even guess. You see, father never bought me a Christmas present before—he always left mother to choose. He said she knew more about such things than he did."

"Then ye can take my word for it, if it's the first one he's ever got ye 'twill be the best ye ever had." Barney spoke with conviction, while Johanna leaned over David's chair and put a loving arm about his shoulder.

"There's some virtue in losing them ye love for a bit, after all, if it makes one o' them think about ye and Christmas. Sure, there's nothing better in life to put by in your memory than rare thoughts and fine letters. And, I'm mortal glad, myself, there's something good coming to ye, laddy, from over yonder, for many's the time Barney and I have been afeared 'twas a lonesome Christmas ye'd be finding up here."

And to the great surprise of every one, David included, David answered cheerfully:

48

"I don't believe it's half bad. Maybe there's more Christmas round than we know."

The orange sun had paled to yellow and climbed half the length of the tallest pine from the crest of the hill when David, bundled and furred, adjusted his skees outside the lodge door. Carefully he pushed his way over the level stretch of new snow, for one never knew with new snow just how far one might go down before striking the crust of the old. A few yards beyond the nearest clump of evergreen he stopped. From this point the mountain sloped down on three sides; the fourth carried over the ridge to the neighboring hill. Here David could look down on the encircling valley; and though the snow lay unbroken everywhere save on the road leading straight down to the "crossing" and the village beyond, he could almost vision paths branching out from where he stood and leading down to the three inhabited dwellings on the mountain's side.

Which way should he go? Where would he first strike his trail for Christmas? Would he follow the road or one of the invisible paths? He asked this silently at first, and then aloud, as if there might be

49

some one near by to hear; and the answer came in the form of a little gray furry coat, a pair of alert ears and a long, bushy tail. Yes, David knew in a twinkling it was the locked-out fairy, come to keep his promise. He did not come close enough for David to see the round, roguish face under the squirrel cap; but he sat up and twitched his head in the direction of the road as if he were saying:

"Come along, David, ye couldn't be wishing for a braver day to go Christmas-hunting. Have ye fetched along your fowling piece and your ammunition? For 'tis rare sport, I promise ye, a hundred times better than hunting your furred or feathered brothers. Come along!" And away he hopped down the road toward the crossing.

David followed, as you or I would, and never stopped till the fairy led him straight to the flagman's hut and disappeared himself behind the drifts beyond the track. Without a moment's hesitation David turned the knob of the door and walked in.

The hut was a small one-room affair, bare, but clean. The walls were whitewashed and held an array of flags and lanterns, maps and time-tables. An air-tight stove glowed red at one end of the room, and beside it, with his feet on the hob, tilted back in his chair, sat the flagman puffing away at an old meerschaum pipe. He was plainly surprised to see his visitor. His feet came back to the floor with a bang, his pipe came out of his mouth, and he stared at David incredulously for a full minute. Then the ends of his grizzled mustache bristled upward, his mouth opened and twisted the same way, while his eyes seemed to drop downward to meet it, all the time growing bluer and more friendly. David took the whole effect to be a smile of welcome and he responded with out-stretched mittened hand.

"Good morning, sir. It's a—it's a grand day!"

The knotted fist of the flagman accepted the mitten and shook it warmly.

"Vell—vell—it ees the knabelein from the hilltop come to see old Fritz Grossman. A child again—it ees goot!"

He reached for a little stool, the only other piece of furniture in the room, and pushed it toward David.

"Come—take off the greatcoat and seet down. It

ees long since old Fritz has had a child to see him. In summer they come sometime from the big hotel, and from the veelage they used to many come. But now—ach! Now, since the war, eet ees deefferent. Now I am the enemy—the German—and here every one hate the German!"

David felt about for something to say and repeated something he had once remarked: "War makes enemies."

"Ach, ja. But here there ees no war. Here we should all be Americans, and not hate peebles for the country where they were born. Gott in Himmel, can there not be one country kept clean of the hate!"

The blue eyes suddenly grew wet, and he blinked them hard and fast to keep the wetness from spilling over into disgraceful tears.

"Tsa! Old Fritz grow more old woman every day! I not mind but for the children not coming; and this time here and no little tongues to beg tales of the Krist Kindlein and the Weihnachtsman from old Fritz."

David drew closer and laid a friendly hand on the flagman's knee.

52

"I'd like to hear one—I'd like bully well to hear one!"

The flagman croaked gleefully deep down in his throat.

"Zo—but first—I know—the knabelein has a stomach got. All have."

He rose stiffly and reached back of the stove to where hung his own great bear-coat. From the pocket he brought out a large red apple and handed it to David.

"There, eat. And you shall hear the tale of anodder apple, a Chreestmas apple."

The flagman tilted back his chair again and replaced his feet upon the hob. David sat with elbows on knees and ate slowly. There was no sound but the occasional dropping of coals in the stove and the soft, deep guttural of the flagman's voice. And here is the story as he told it to David—only the broken German accent and the dropping coals are missing.

Once on a time there lived in Germany a little clock-maker by the name of Hermann Joseph. He lived in one little room with a bench for his work,

53

and a chest for his wood, and his tools, and a cupboard for dishes, and a trundle-bed under the bench.
Besides these there was a stool, and that was all—
excepting the clocks. There were hundreds of
clocks: little and big, carved and plain, some with
wooden faces and some with porcelain ones—shelf
clocks, cuckoo clocks, clocks with chimes and clocks
without; and they all hung on the walls, covering
them quite up. In front of his one little window
there was a little shelf, and on this Hermann put all
his best clocks to show the passers-by. Often they
would stop and look and some one would cry:

"See, Hermann Joseph has made a new clock.
It is finer than any of the rest!"

Then if it happened that anybody was wanting a
clock he would come in and buy it.

I said Hermann was a little clock-maker. That
was because his back was bent and his legs were
crooked, which made him very short and funny to
look at. But there was no kinder face than his in
all the city, and the children loved him. Whenever
a toy was broken or a doll had lost an arm or a leg

54

or an eye its careless mütterchen would carry it straight to Hermann's little shop.

"The kindlein needs mending," she would say. "Canst thou do it now for me?"

And whatever work Hermann was doing he would always put it aside to mend the broken toy or doll, and never a pfennig would he take for the mending.

"Go spend it for sweetmeats, or, better still, put it by till Christmas-time. 'Twill get thee some happiness then, maybe," he would always say.

Now it was the custom in that long ago for those who lived in the city to bring gifts to the great cathedral on Christmas and lay them before the Holy Mother and Child. People saved all through the year that they might have something wonderful to bring on that day; and there was a saying among them that when a gift was brought that pleased the Christ-child more than any other He would reach down from Mary's arms and take it. This was but a saying, of course. The old Herr Graff, the oldest man in the city, could not remember that it had ever really happened; and many there were who laughed

55

at the very idea. But children often talked about it, and the poets made beautiful verses about it; and often when a rich gift was placed beside the altar the watchers would whisper among themselves, "Perhaps now we shall see the miracle."

Those who had no gifts to bring went to the cathedral just the same on Christmas Eve to see the gifts of the others and hear the carols and watch the burning of the waxen tapers. The little clock-maker was one of these. Often he was stopped and some one would ask, "How happens it that you never bring a gift?" Once the bishop himself questioned him: "Poorer than thou have brought offerings to the Child. Where is thy gift?"

Then it was that Hermann had answered: "Wait; some day you shall see. I, too, shall bring a gift some day."

The truth of it was that the little clock-maker was so busy giving away all the year that there was never anything left at Christmas-time. But he had a wonderful idea on which he was working every minute that he could spare time from his clocks. It had taken him years and years; no one knew anything

56

about it but Trude, his neighbor's child, and Trude had grown from a baby into a little house-mother, and still the gift was not finished.

It was to be a clock, the most wonderful and beautiful clock ever made; and every part of it had been fashioned with loving care. The case, the works, the weights, the hands, and the face, all had taken years of labor. He had spent years carving the case and hands, years perfecting the works; and now Hermann saw that with a little more haste and time he could finish it for the coming Christmas. He mended the children's toys as before, but he gave up making his regular clocks, so there were fewer to sell, and often his cupboard was empty and he went supperless to bed. But that only made him a little thinner and his face a little kinder; and meantime the gift clock became more and more beautiful. It was fashioned after a rude stable with rafters, stall, and crib. The Holy Mother knelt beside the manger in which a tiny Christ-child lay, while through the open door the hours came. Three were kings and three were shepherds and three were soldiers and three were angels; and when the hours struck, the figure

57

knelt in adoration before the sleeping Child, while the silver chimes played the "Magnificat."

"Thou seest," said the clock-maker to Trude, "it is not just on Sundays and holidays that we should remember to worship the Krist Kindlein and bring Him gifts—but every day, every hour."

The days went by like clouds scudding before a winter wind and the clock was finished at last. So happy was Hermann with his work that he put the gift clock on the shelf before the little window to show the passers-by. There were crowds looking at it all day long, and many would whisper, "Do you think this can be the gift Hermann has spoken of—his offering on Christmas Eve to the Church?"

The day before Christmas came. Hermann cleaned up his little shop, wound all his clocks, brushed his clothes, and then went over the gift clock again to be sure everything was perfect.

"It will not look meanly beside the other gifts," he thought, happily. In fact he was so happy that he gave away all but one pfennig to the blind beggar who passed his door; and then, remembering that he had eaten nothing since breakfast, he spent that last pfennig for a Christmas apple to eat with a crust of bread he had. These he was putting by in the cupboard to eat after he was dressed, when the door opened and Trude was standing there crying softly.

"Kindlein—kindlein, what ails thee?" And he gathered her into his arms.

" 'Tis the father. He is hurt, and all the money that was put by for the tree and sweets and toys has gone to Herr Doctor. And now, how can I tell the children? Already they have lighted the candle at the window and are waiting for Kriss Kringle to come."

The clock-maker laughed merrily.

"Come, come, little one, all will be well. Hermann will sell a clock for thee. Some house in the city must need a clock; and in a wink we shall have money enough for the tree and the toys. Go home and sing."

He buttoned on his greatcoat and, picking out the best of the old clocks, he went out. He went first to the rich merchants, but their houses were full of clocks; then to the journeymen, but they said his clock was old-fashioned. He even stood on the corners of the streets and in the square, crying, "A clock —a good clock for sale," but no one paid any attention to him. At last he gathered up his courage and went to the Herr Graff himself.

"Will your Excellency buy a clock?" he said, trembling at his own boldness. "I would not ask, but it is Christmas and I am needing to buy happiness for some children."

The Herr Graff smiled.

"Yes, I will buy a clock, but not that one. I will pay a thousand gulden for the clock thou hast had in thy window these four days past."

"But, your Excellency, that is impossible!" And poor Hermann trembled harder than ever.

"Poof! Nothing is impossible. That clock or none. Get thee home and I will send for it in half an hour, and pay thee the gulden."

The little clock-maker stumbled out.

"Anything but that—anything but that!" he kept mumbling over and over to himself on his way home. But as he passed the neighbor's house he saw the children at the window with their lighted candle and he heard Trude singing.

*The Door Opened and Trude
Stood There, Crying Softly*

And so it happened that the servant who came from the Herr Graff carried the gift clock away with him; but the clock-maker would take but five of the thousand gulden in payment. And as the servant disappeared up the street the chimes commenced to ring from the great cathedral, and the streets suddenly became noisy with the many people going thither, bearing their Christmas offerings.

"I have gone empty-handed before," said the little clock-maker, sadly. "I can go empty-handed once again." And again he buttoned up his greatcoat.

As he turned to shut his cupboard door behind him his eyes fell on the Christmas apple and an odd little smile crept into the corners of his mouth and lighted his eyes.

"It is all I have—my dinner for two days. I will carry that to the Christ-child. It is better, after all, than going empty-handed."

How full of peace and beauty was the great cathedral when Hermann entered it! There were a thousand tapers burning and everywhere the sweet scent of the Christmas greens—and the laden altar before the Holy Mother and Child. There were richer gifts than had been brought for many years: marvelously wrought vessels from the greatest silver-smiths; cloth of gold and cloth of silk brought from the East by the merchants; poets had brought their songs illuminated on rolls of heavy parchment; painters had brought their pictures of saints and the Holy Family; even the King himself had brought his crown and scepter to lay before the Child. And after all these offerings came the little clock-maker, walking slowly down the long, dim aisle, holding tight to his Christmas apple.

The people saw him and a murmur rose, hummed a moment indistinctly through the church and then grew clear and articulate:

"Shame! See, he is too mean to bring his clock! He hoards it as a miser hoards his gold. See what he brings! Shame!"

The words reached Hermann and he stumbled on blindly, his head dropped forward on his breast, his hands groping the way. The distance seemed interminable. Now he knew he was past the seats; now his feet touched the first step, and there were seven to climb to the altar. Would his feet never reach the top?

"One, two, three," he counted to himself, then tripped and almost fell. "Four, five, six." He was nearly there. There was but one more.

The murmur of shame died away and in its place rose one of wonder and awe. Soon the words became intelligible:

"The miracle! It is the miracle!"

The people knelt in the big cathedral; the bishop raised his hands in prayer. And the little clockmaker, stumbling to the last step, looked up through dim eyes and saw the Child leaning toward him, far down from Mary's arms, with hands outstretched to take his gift.

That night, back in the kitchen of the lodge after supper, David told the story again to Johanna and Barney. And when he had finished he saw them looking strangely at each other.

"To think," said Johanna, thoughtfully, "we've been living here for two years and we never got so much from the old man. And who'd have thought

63

to find such a tale bundled up in an old bunch of heathen rags and language like him?"

"Maybe, now, he's not a heathen at all," laughed Barney.

And the others laughed with him.

V. The Pathway to Uncle Joab and a New Santa Claus

NO fresh snow fell through the night, and when David slipped his feet into the skee straps at the lodge door next morning he was rejoiced to find that the snow had packed and crusted a little since the day before, which meant better going. Again he made for the clump of evergreens and again he stood at the pinnacle of the ways and wondered which he would take.

"I might count," he laughed aloud—"I might count them out." And with that he fell into the school-boy doggerel, nearly as old as boyhood itself: "Eeny—meeny—miny—mo. Catch—a nigger—by the—"

He came to a sudden stop. In the direction of the lumber camp, where the evergreens marked the beginning of the road, he had caught a glimpse of a gray squirrel. Was it a real squirrel this time, or was it the locked-out fairy again? There was not a minute to be lost. He must find out.

Over the unbroken snow he slid, balancing himself carefully when he came to the hummocks made by the wind or fallen trees, his eyes coming back constantly to the little gray figure before him. It was sitting erect now, under a green bough, apparently busy investigating the contents of a pine cone. But just as David had made up his mind that this time it was a real squirrel, up went the furry paw to an ear in unmistakable salute, just as the locked-out fairy had done when he hopped from the window-ledge of the lodge. Then, with ears set back and tail out straight behind, the squirrel flew down the hill. Away went David after him, the tassel of his toboggan-cap out as straight as the squirrel's tail.

Never was there such a race. They dodged trees and fallen branches; they leaped drifts; they spun like tops around the curves. Sometimes David was so close upon the fairy's heels that he could almost have touched him with the end of his steering-cane, but the next moment he generally lost his balance and slipped a skee, and head over heels he would go in the crusty snow. When he righted himself the fairy was always yards ahead, sitting with his shoulders all hunched up as if he were laughing silently at David's tumble. So exciting was the whole race that David entirely forgot his destination until he suddenly found himself almost bumping a corner of one of the lumber cabins, and the fairy nowhere in sight.

He stopped a minute for breath and to wonder what he would do, when he heard the soft, silvery notes of a violin. The music was coming from inside that very cabin, and a voice was humming softly as well. David moved round to one of the windows, hoping he might be tall enough to look in, but the snow had drifted away from that side and he missed the ledge by several inches. It occurred to him, however, that if the snow had drifted from this end it had probably drifted toward the other. He would try it, at any rate. Round the cabin he went, and, sure enough, there the snow had piled up half-way to the window and David found he could look in comfortably.

There was a great fire blazing inside, and by it sat an old negro with the whitest hair and beard David had ever seen. A violin was tucked under his chin and slowly and lovingly he was bowing the melody from it, while one foot patted the time on the floor and a plaintive, mellow voice put words to the music. David listened for the words and caught them:

"Yeah come-a-No-ah—a-stumblin' tru de dark,
  Wif hammah an' wif nails-to-a-build hisself an ark.
  An'-a-yeah come de an'mals-two-a-by two,
  De Yippo-ma-pot'mus—an' de kick-kangaroo."

The bowing suddenly stopped and David was conscious of a pair of very white eyeballs looking at him through the glass. For the space of a breath or more David was not at all sure that he wanted to get any nearer that strange, bent old figure. He was almost sure that he did not want to go inside. Not that he was afraid. Oh no, indeed! He was not in the least bit afraid; there was nothing to be afraid of. Even Johanna had not said anything harmful about the old cook at the lumber camp. Nevertheless, there was something mysterious, something not altogether inviting about that inky-black face with the white hair and rolling eyeballs.

David was speedily withdrawing himself, having decided that there was great virtue in distance, when

68

he heard the creak of the cabin door. In a trice the old negro, fiddle in hand, appeared around the corner.

"Wha you goin', honey?" There was unmistakable regret over David's retreating figure.

"Why—why, I'm just going back where I came from."

"Wha you come from?"

David pointed upward and the old darky nodded comprehendingly.

" 'Pears to me dat am a long way fer a li'l' boy to come an' den turn 'bout an' go right home. Come in, honey, an' Uncle Joab 'll play you somethin' lively on de ole fiddle."

David hesitated, but only for an instant. There was something too lonely and appealing about the man to be denied. David was still not at all sure that he wanted to go, even while he was following the lumber cook round to the door.

It was surprisingly cozy and cheerful inside, perhaps because of the open fire, the strips of pine cones, husked corn, and bunches of colored berries that decorated the walls and rafters. Uncle

69

Joab caught David's wondering, curious gaze, and he chuckled.

"Yas, dat's pop-corn, honey. An' I reckon Uncle Joab 'll have some a-poppin' for you over dese yeah coals in a jiffy."

He mounted stiffly the hewn, polished stump that did service for a stool and pulled down two of the ears. From the corner of the fireplace he brought a corn-popper and, sitting down, he commenced to shell the corn by rubbing the ears together. David drew up a chair near by and watched him with growing interest. When the corn was shelled Uncle Joab raked away the unburned wood from the fire, leaving a bed of the red coals. Over this he held the corn, shaking the popper gently from side to side. In less time than it takes for the telling sounded the snap-snap-snap of the bursting kernels, and in a moment more Uncle Joab had turned the snowy contents into an earthen bowl and laid it on David's knee with a small dish of salt and the invitation to "Go ahead." Then he took up his fiddle again and played the promised music.

It was a jig, such a rollicking, care-free jig that

70

before it was finished David found himself wondering how in the world he ever hesitated about coming in. Why, here was nothing but another boy like himself, a boy grown old before he had grown up.

"Like dat corn, honey? Wall, you come along yeah 'round Chris'mus an' Uncle Joab 'll make you some m'lasses balls."

A sigh escaped with the promise.

"Lordy—Chris'mus—yeah! Doan't seem like I done hab any Chris'mus sence I left ole Virginy. Seems like it done froze stiff 'fo' ever it got to dese yeah parts."

David laughed at the old man's humor. It had seemed just that way to him a few days ago.

"Couldn't we thaw it out?" he asked.

" 'Twould take a monstrous lot o' warm feelin's, honey, an' kind folks, I reckon. An' you'd not find 'em a-hangin' 'round loose yeah in de wintah. Why, dere's no more 'n a han'ful of us, all measured an' mixted; an' as fur as I know dere's not one a-speakin' to another."

David shook his head solemnly.

"That's not much like Christmas, is it, Uncle

71

Joab? Not much 'good-will' when you don't know your neighbors."

The old darky grunted, then he chuckled.

" 'Pears to me it's de critters dat get on yeah more folksy den de real folks—an' dat put me in mind of a story my mammy used to tell me when I was your size."

David beamed.

"Will you tell it, Uncle Joab?"

"Co'se I'll tell it, honey." And putting the fiddle down beside his chair he began:

"I reckon you think dat de jolly ole saint wif de red nose an' de dimple somewhas 'twixt his mouf an' his ears only 'members de chillun at Chris'mus. An' dat's not de trouf. Dere was one Chris'mus long time ago, after Pharoe's daughter found Moses in de bull-grass an' 'fo' Christoper Columbus went a-sailin' 'round to find dis yeah country, dat ole man Santy gib a Chris'mus to de critters. An' dis was de way of it.

"In dose days dere warn't de chilluns dere is now. Dey warn't so plentiful an' dey warn't so perticular;

72

an' each one warn't lookin' fer a whole shed full o' toys jest fer hisself. No, sir, honey! He was bustin' wif tickle if he got one gif' an' some barley sugar. An' what's more, dey warn't so pernicity 'bout what dey got. De dolls didn't have to walk an' talk an' act like real folks an' de trains didn't have to go by demselves. An' everything bein' so comf'able an' easy, ole Santy could tote de pack o' toys 'round hisself on his back an' be home a good two hour 'fo' daylight, wif nothin' to do de rest o' de day but set 'round an' think.

"Wall, in dose days, honey, de folks doan't pester de critters wif workin' dem all de time. No, sir! Dey work dem when dey need dem, an' de balance o' de time de critters trope 'round free an' easy-like. Folks wasn't cotchin' de cur'ous ones to put in de menageries an' de circuses, nor de furry ones to trim up de ladies wif. Times was pleasant an' comf'able fer every one.

"Now it transmigrate one day when ole Santy was a-settin' an' rumminatin' dat he fotch up his thoughts on de critters, an' he says to hisself, says he:

"'Pears like dey has a right to Chris'mus same

73

as de folks. Dey minds dere bus'ness, an' dey works an' dey plays de same, an' dey had dere share in dat fust Chris'mus when de li'l' Lordie was born—same as de folks. Didn't de donkey carry Mary to Befle-hem? Didn't de mully-cow gib her manger for de li'l' Lordie to sleep in? Didn't de cock crow de news to St. Stephen? An' how do yer reckon de Wise Men could ha' toted dere presents 'cross de sand if it hadn't been fer dem cam'ls?'

"Yas, sir, honey! Ole Santy was right. De crit-ters had as much right to Chris'mus as de folks, an' ole Santy poun' his knee an' swear he gwine to gib dem one.

"So de ole saint he begun fer to study an' to study what he gwine to do fer de critters. He can't come down dere chimbleys 'ca'se dey 'ain't got no houses; an' he can't fill dere stockin's 'ca'se dey doan't wear none; an' he can't fotch dem barley candy 'ca'se dey doan't eat it. Wall, he set dere an' study twell his brain 'mos' bustin' an' bime-by he fotch up wif an idea.

"'I know what I'll do,' says ole Santy, says he. 'Dem critters is sure to be like folks; dere's certain to be a lot dat ain't satisfied wif dere pussonalities. Now I'm gwine to trim up a Chris'mus tree wif a lot o' odd tails, an' ears, an' wings, an' legs, an' sech-like, an' any o' de critters dat ain't satisfied can choose jes' what dey want. Dat's what I'm gwine to do,' says ole Santy.

"Wall, thinkin' was doin'. An' by de time Chris'mus come along dat ole saint had de mos' cur'os, hetromologous collection o' an'mal parts you ever done hear tell about. He sent word by de birds all over de world fer de critters to come to a Chris'mus celebration at de fust fir-tree dis side o' de North Pole. 'Fo' dey git dere ole Santy had it all trimmed up wif his presents; an' when de critters trope up dey sure was bustin' wif s'prize when dey see all de tails an' wings an' legs hangin' dere.

"An' de an'mals! Bless your heart, honey, you never see such a camp-meetin'! Dere was elephants an' tigers an' lions an' yippopot'musses an' rabbits an' 'possums an' mouses—every livin' kind. An' all de birds dat clip de air an' all de fish dat swum de sea. Dey all come lopin' up wif dere purtiest manners on; an' dey scrape an' dey bow an' ax after ole

Missus Santy an' de chilluns. When dey'd axed an' scraped all 'round, ole Santy says, says he:

" 'Now any o' you-all critters dat want fer to change yer pussonalities can jes' step right up an' choose somethin' new,' says he.

"Everybody was mighty bashful at fust. Dey all tried to hide behind dere neighbors an' look like dey was puffectly satisfied wif dere looks an' dere habits. But bime-by a squeaky li'l' voice calls out:

" 'If you please, Ole Man Santy, I'd like a pair o' dem li'l' brown wings, an' thank you mighty much.'

"Santy look down an' see it was one o' de li'l' mouses speakin'; an' he reach up an' take from de tree a cunnin' pair o' li'l' wings an' fastened dem on tight. An' de next minute dat sassy li'l' mouse went flippin' an' floppin' into de air same as if he'd been born wif wings. An' ever since, honey, he an' his chilluns have been flyin' 'stead o' creepin'."

"Did he turn into a bat, Uncle Joab?" David asked.

"Sure. What else you 'spec' he could turn into? Wall, de nex' to walk up was Bre'r Rabbit. He had a lot to say 'bout his ears bein' so short he couldn't

*"Please, Ole Man Santy, I'd Like
a Pair o' Dem Li'l'
Brown Wings"*

hear 'nough, an' his tail bein' so long he couldn't fetch up on it com'fably in de brier patch. He'd be powerful pleased if Santy 'd gib him bigger ears an' take away his tail. Dis made de ole saint chuckle; an' he fotch down de biggest pair he can find an' put dem on, an' den he twist off de rabbit's long, bushy tail. When de other critters see what transmigrate dey like to bu'st dere sides wif laughin'; an' dis scare Bre'r Rabbit so dat he lay back his ears so he can't hear so well, an' he lope off to hide his confusi'n in de brier patch. An' dere you'll find him hidin' to dis yeah day, honey."

David laughed.

"And were there any more who weren't satisfied?"

"Didn't I tell you de critters were like folks? Bre'r Rabbit hadn't more 'n cleared de Chris'mus tree when de squirrel sings out:

" 'If you please, Mr. Santy, I'd like Brudder Rabbit's tail. I'd like Brudder Rabbit's tail.'

" ' 'Twon't fit you,' says de beaver. 'It's three sizes too big.'

" 'No, it ain't! No, it ain't! No, it ain't!' An' de squirrel carry on so scan'lously dat ole Santy

77

'bliged to gib him de tail to keep him quiet. But, bless your heart, honey, you know as well as I do dat dat tail am no fit for dat squirrel!

"By dis time de critters was nigh over dere bashfulness, an' dey was clamorin' for what dey wanted. De leopard say his coat too yaller, an' he'd like some nice, stylish black spots to tone it down. Den de zebra say stripes was more stylish dis year den spots, an' he'd 'low he'd like stripes. De elephant say his feet too big to pick up things handy, an' he'd like somethin' extra to pick up things wif.

"Dis set de rest o' de critters to 'sputin' whar de elephant have room on his pussonality fer anythin' extra; an' while dey 'sputin' ole Santy sit still an' study. Bime-by he says, says he:

" 'De only spare room am on de end o' your nose. If you want to have it dere, say so!'

"De elephant he say so. So Santy take one o' dese yeah suckers, left over from a debil-fish, an' he stick it squar' in de middle o' de elephant's nose. He stick it so hard, an' he stick it so fast, dat it hasn't come loose dese thousand o' years.

"Wall, dat certainly was a busy Chris'mus fer de

78

ole saint. He was fixin' tails an' legs an' ears an' wings 'most all day. De beaver he gets de sulks 'ca'se de squirrel's got Bre'r Rabbit's tail an' he want it. De rest o' de critters try to coax him to take somethin' else, but 'pears like he crazy fer somethin' behind. He took to moanin' an' wailin' 'ca'se he can't get what he wants twell bime-by he nat'rally gets ole Santy plumb wore out.

" 'Look yeah,' says ole Santy, says he. 'You's so sot on havin' somethin' behind, 'pears like I'd hab to gib you somethin' diff'rent an' distinguishin'.' An' wif dat de ole saint claps on him one o' dem flappers dat he'd made fer de li'l' seals to walk on. An' it's been hangin' to de back o' de beaver ever since.

"At las' all de critters were satisfied 'ceptin' de dog an' de horse an' de reindeer.

" 'What you want?' says ole Santy to de dog.

" 'I want faithfulness,' says de dog; an' Santy gib it to him.

" 'What you want?' he says to de horse.

" 'I want wisdom,' says de horse; an' Santy whisper it into his ear.

" 'Now what you want?' he says last of all to de reindeer.

" 'I want to be your servant an' lib always wif you,' says de reindeer. An' from dat minute to dis de reindeer an' his chilluns have been totin' fer ole Santy.

"An' you listen yeah, honey. If you borrow Bre'r Rabbit's ears to hear wif dis Chris'mus p'raps you'll cotch de tromp o' de reindeer's hoofs an' de jingle o' his bells as he totes ole Santy through de night."

David laughed happily.

"That's a bully story, Uncle Joab, just a bully one!"

The old man chuckled appreciatively.

"Mebbe it's good enough to fotch a li'l' boy back some other day to see dis ole nigger."

Johanna and Barney had to hear the story over twice before David went to bed that night. They seemed to like it as much as David had liked it.

"It must get pretty lonesome for the poor man, stormy days and long winter nights with no company but that old fiddle," mused Johanna at last.

"Faith, I wouldn't be minding a bit o' that same company, myself, some night," laughed Barney. " 'Tis a sorry time since I've heard any good fiddling."

But David did not say anything. He was looking deep into the fire and thinking very hard.

VI. The Locked-out Fairy Again Leads the Way and David Hears of a Christmas Promise

DAVID was already beginning to feel very rich in Christmas as he climbed to the crest of the hill the next morning. Yes, the locked-out fairy was right. Real Christmas lay in the hearts and memories of people, and he was sure he was storing up some in his own to last for always.

It was still four days before Christmas, yet he felt all the warm glow of excitement, all the eagerness, all the gladness, that usually attended the very day itself. He was beginning to think that instead of one Christmas he was finding a whole week of it, and for a little boy who had had loneliness fastened to his heels like a shadow for so long the feeling was very wonderful. Not that he did not miss father and mother just the same, but they no longer seemed so far away. There were minutes when he could think them quite close, when they seemed to have a share in all he was doing and thinking, and when that happens with anyone we love loneliness vanishes like a shadow at midday.

There were but two paths left for him that morning to choose between—the path leading to the trapper's and the one to the "lunger's." It was not a particularly cheery day. The sky was a leaden gray —a hue forecasting snow before day's end. The wind was biting and raw, and had there not been a quest afoot David would have been glad to stay near home and share Barney's cheerful company. As it was, he had about made up his mind that he should choose the trapper. He knew as little about him as he had known of the others, and he pictured a big, gruff, hairy man something like his old Grimm illustration of Bluebeard. But for all that, he seemed more alluring on such a day than a "lunger."

David very much hoped that the locked-out fairy would be there to take him the way he had chosen to go. He wanted not only the guidance of the fairy, but he wished to see him close again and talk with him. He was looking about for signs when his eyes

83

swept the snow at his feet and there he found the trail laid for him. As far as eye could reach there were the tiny sharp prints of a squirrel's foot, and they led, not down the hillside to the trapper's hut, but, straight as a stone drops, to the foot-hill beyond, where the "lunger's" cottage stood.

David heaved a sigh of disappointment. He would so much rather have gone the other way; but of what use is a fairy counselor and guide if one does not follow his trail? So with something very near to a flagging courage David pushed his way slowly after the tiny footprints.

He missed the exhilaration of the sunshine and air and excitement of the previous days. Somehow he felt this time was going to be a failure and he shrank from facing it; moreover, he thought of what he might have to tell Johanna and Barney afterward, around the fire. A moment before he had felt so rich in the feeling of Christmas. And now, was he going to find an unpleasant memory to take away from the good ones?

There was no sign of life about the little cottage on the foot-hill. The sleeping-porch was deserted, the windows were heavily curtained, the snow was piled up high and unbroken about the door; even the roadway beyond, which led down the other side to the village, was smooth and crusted, showing that no one had come or gone from the house since the last fall of snow.

"It looks awfully gloomy and deserted," thought David. "The 'lunger' must have gone away or died!"

The last was a dreadfully dreary thought, and it almost turned David's feet on the very threshold, in spite of the fairy's trail. But the memory of the day before held him back. How nearly he had come to losing a bit of Christmas just because an old white-haired negro had looked at him suddenly through a window! He would mark himself as a quitter and a " 'fraid-cat" for all time if he ever let such a thing happen again. And what would the boys on the block think of him?

With heroic boldness David pushed his skees up to the baseboard of the door and hammered hard on the brass knocker. Once, twice, three times he knocked. Then he heard soft feet inside and the

85

turning of the key in the lock. In another minute the door opened, letting in a generous fall of snow and disclosing a tall, oldish woman in black, with very black hair and big, sorrowful black eyes.

"Madre de Díos!" she exclaimed in a soft voice full of surprised wonder. "A niño—here, in this freeze country!"

"If you please," began David, politely, "I came— I came—"

But he did not finish. For the life of him he could not have told just why he had come.

"Entre, come!" And the woman drew him in and closed the door behind him. "A boy! It may be that it will put again the heart in Alfredo to see a boy. Come, chico!"

She opened another door at the end of a hall and led him into a bare, cold, cheerless room. Half a dozen black bentwood chairs stood with backs against the walls; the two rockers of the same faced each other at opposite sides of the fireplace; and between them stretched a cot covered with heavy blankets. A half-hearted fire burned on the hearth,

86

and watching it listlessly from the cot lay a boy about twice his age, David thought.

"See, Alfredo! See chicito mío, who come here," the woman called. And the sick youth turned his head slowly to look at them.

David saw a thin, colorless face with great, black eyes. They had the same look that was in the woman's eyes, only the woman did not look sick, only sad. As the boy saw David he smiled in a pleased, surprised way, and held out a thin, white hand in welcome. But the hand was so thin David was almost ashamed to put out his own broad, brown little fist to take it. He compromised by leaving on his mitten—and he shook it very gently.

"Ah, it is good," said the boy, simply. "I am glad to see you."

"Thank you," David beamed. He was glad he had come. For here there were things that he could do, and first of all he'd tackle the fire.

"It's this way," he explained as he slipped out of his outside things. "I'm spending the winter up on the hill, in the hotel lodge. It's been getting sort of lonesome there lately since winter set in, so I thought

87

—I—it seemed sort of nice to come around and look up some of the neighbors." David finished out of breath.

Alfredo and his mother exchanged glances.

"That is good," said the boy at last. "You are the first one, and we, too, have been what you call 'lonesome.'"

"I'm awfully sorry." And this time David held out the unmittened fist. "Say, do you mind if I build up that fire a little? It looks sort of—sick."

"Ah!" The woman held up protesting hands. "Alfredo is too sick but to lie still. And I—what do I know about building fires in open places with wood? It is only the carbon I know, and the shut stove. And when our servant leave us three—four day ago and no one ever comes near to us I think then that we die of the cold before long time."

Tears of utter despair showed in the woman's eyes; and David found his own growing sympathetically moist.

"Oh, no! Barney wouldn't let that happen—not to anyone."

It really was dreadful to find a sick boy and a wo-

88

man alone—strangers in this country—with the cold and the loneliness to fight.

"Now you tell me where the wood is, and I'll have a cracker-jack fire in a minute. Barney's showed me how. I can make 'em burn even when the wood's damp." David did not finish without a tinge of pride in his tone.

He made several trips to the little back room beyond the kitchen which served as woodshed, and in a few minutes he had a generous stack of logs and kindlings beside the hearth and a roaring fire blazing up the big chimney. The glow and warmth lit up Alfredo's cheeks and kindled a new life in the woman's eyes. Such a little thing it takes sometimes to put the hearts back in people.

"Now, if you want me to, I'll just fill up the kitchen stove and the one in the hall. It's really too cold here for anyone," he ended, apologetically.

The woman accepted his offer, mutely grateful; and when both stoves had finally responded to his coaxings and were cheerfully crackling and sending out the much-needed heat, David came back to the open fire and drew up one of the rockers.

89

"It is a good niño, eh, Alfredito?" said the woman, softly.

David wriggled uncomfortably.

"Say—I'll tell you about the flagman, and Uncle Joab at the lumber camp. Want me to?"

The offer was made as a cloak to his embarrassment; but the next moment, as he launched into his narrative of the two previous days, he had forgotten everything but the tales he had to tell and the interest of his listeners.

When he had finished, David was surprised to see the change in the faces of the two. For the first time they seemed really alive and warm, inside and out. Moreover, they looked happy, strangely happy.

"We had almost forgot, chico mío," the mother said, stroking one of the thin, white hands, "that comes now the Natividad. Ah, who would think to find it here in this freeze country!"

"We are South-Americans," the boy explained. "And down there it is summer now, with the oranges ripe, and the piña growing and the air full of the sweetness from the coffee-fields in bloom and the jasmine and mariposa. We did not know such cold

90

could be—or so much snow. Eh, madre?" And the boy smiled wanly.

"But how did you come way up here from your country? Was it the—" David left the question unfinished.

The boy nodded.

"I came first to be in one of your fine universities. Many South-Americans come here for their education. But before many months I take the cough, and it is then no use to go back to our country. We blow out there like a candle in the wind."

The mother went on.

"But the great American doctor say here there is a chance in the mountains, if he can stand the winter. And oh, at first he grow much better! We see the good health coming. But now, the great cold, the heart-hunger, the alone being, it seem to take his strength. I fear—"

"Hush, madre! This is not good cheer for a guest."

David felt his cheeks burn with the sudden tenderness in the boy's look.

"Come, madre," he went on, "have we not also a

tale of Christmas, of the Natividad, to give away?"

"There is that one I have told you a thousand times —the one my mother told me when I was a niña, home in Spain. The tale of the Tres Reyes and the Christmas promise."

The boy sighed happily.

"There is no better tale in all Spain. Tell it, madre, to our friend here."

And so this was how the third bit of Christmas came to David, by way of a locked-out fairy, a re-kindled fire, and a stranger from the far South.

When the Christ-child was born in Bethlehem of Judea, long years ago, three kings rode out of the East on their camels, bearing gifts to Him. They followed the star until at last they came to the manger where He lay, a little, new-born baby. Kneeling down, they put their gifts beside Him: gold, frankincense, and myrrh; they kissed the hem of the little white mantle that He wore, and blessed Him. Then the kings rode away to the East again, but before ever they went they whispered a promise to the Christ-child.

92

And the promise? You shall hear it as the kings gave it to the Christ-child, long years ago.

"As long as there be children on the earth, on every Christmas Eve we three kings shall ride on camels, even as we rode to Thee this night; and even as we bore Thee gifts so shall we bear gifts to every child in memory of Thee—thou holy Babe of Bethlehem!"

In Spain they have remembered what the Christmas kings promised, and when Christmas Eve comes each child puts his sapatico—his little shoe—between the gratings of the window that they may know a child is in that house and leave a gift.

Often the shoe is filled with grass for the camels, and a plate of dates and figs is left beside it, for the children know the kings have far to go and may be hungry.

At day's end bands of children march out of the city gates, going to meet the kings. But it always grows dark before they come. The children are afraid upon the lonely road and hurry back to their homes, where the good madres hear them say one prayer to the Nene Jesu, as they call the Christ-child,

93

and then put them to bed to dream of the Christmas kings.

Long, long ago there lived in Spain, in the crowded part of a great city, an old woman called Doña Josefa. The street in which she lived was little and narrow, so narrow that if you leaned out of the window of Doña Josefa's house you could touch with your finger-tips the house across the way, and when you looked above your head the sky seemed but a string of blue, tying the houses all together. The sun never found its way into this little street.

The people who lived here were very poor, as you may guess; Doña Josefa was poor, likewise. But in one thing she was very rich—she knew more stories than there were feast-days in the year, and that is a great many. Whenever there came a moment free from work, when Doña Josefa had no water to fetch from the public well, nor gold to stitch upon the altar cloth for the Church of Santa María del Rosario, then she would run out of her house into the street and call:

"Niños, niños, come quickly! Here is a story waiting for you."

And the children would come flying like the gray palomas when corn is thrown for them in the Plaza. Ah, how many children there were in that little street! There was José and Miguel, and the niños of Enrique, the cobbler, Alfredito and Juana and Esperanza; and the little twin sisters of Pancho, the peddler; and Angela, María Teresa, Pedro, Edita, and many more. Last of all there were Manuel and Rosita. They had no father, and their mother was a lavandera who stood all day on the banks of the river outside the city, washing clothes.

When Doña Josefa had called the children from all the doorways and the dark corners she would sit down in the middle of the street and gather them about her. This was safe because the street was far too narrow to allow a horse or wagon to pass through. Sometimes a donkey would slowly pick its way along, or a stupid goat come searching for things to eat, but that was all.

It happened on the day before Christmas that Doña Josefa had finished her work and sat, as usual, with the children about her.

"To-day you shall have a Christmas story," she

95

said, and then she told them of the three kings and the promise they had made the Christ-child.

"And is it so—do the kings bring presents to the children now?" Miguel asked.

Doña Josefa nodded her head.

"Yes."

"Then why have they never left us one? The three kings never pass this street on Christmas Eve. Why is it, doña?"

"Perhaps it is because we have no shoes to hold their gifts," said Angela.

And this is true. The poor children of Spain go barefooted, and often never have a pair of shoes till they grow up.

Manuel had listened silently to the others, but now he pulled the sleeve of Doña Josefa's gown with coaxing fingers:

"I know why it is the kings bring no gifts to us. See, the street; it is too small; their camels could not pass between the door-steps here. The kings must ride where the streets are broad and smooth and clean, where their long mantles will not be soiled and torn and the camels will not stumble. It is the

96

children in the great streets, the children of the rich, who find presents in their sapaticos on Christmas morning. Is it not so, Doña Josefa?"

And Miguel cried, "Does Manuel speak true—is it only the children of the rich?"

"Ah, chicito mío, it should not be so! When the promise was given to the Nene Jesu there in Bethlehem they said, 'to every child.' Yes, every little child."

"But it is not strange they should forget us here," Manuel insisted. "The little street is hidden in the shadow of the great ones."

Then Rosita spoke, clasping her hands together with great eagerness:

"I know; it is because we have no shoes! That is why they never stop. Perhaps Enrique would lend us the shoes he is mending, just for one night. If we had shoes the kings would surely see that there are little children in the street, and leave a gift for each of us. Come, let us ask Enrique!"

"Madre de Dios, it is a blessed thought!" cried all. And like the flock of gray palomas they swept down the street to the farthest end, where Enrique hammered and stitched away all day on the shoes of the rich children.

Manuel stayed behind with Doña Josefa. When the last pair of little brown feet had disappeared inside the sapatería he said, softly:

"If some one could go out and meet the kings to tell them of this little street, and how the niños here have never had a Christmas gift, do you think they might ride hither to-night?"

Doña Josefa shook her head doubtfully.

"If that were possible— But never have I heard of anyone who met the kings on Christmas Eve."

All day in the city people hurried to and fro. In the great streets flags were waving from the house-tops, and wreaths of laurel, or garlands of heliotrope and mariposa, hung above the open doorways and in the windows. Sweetmeat-sellers were crying their wares; and the Keeper-of-the-City lighted flaming torches to hang upon the gates and city walls. Everywhere was merrymaking and gladness, for not only was this Christmas Eve, but the King of Spain was coming to keep his holiday within the city. Some whispered that he was riding from the North,

98

and with him rode his cousins, the kings of France and Lombardy, and with them were a great following of nobles, knights, and minstrels. Others said the kings rode all alone—it was their wish.

As the sun was turning the cathedral spires to shafts of gold, bands of children, hand in hand, marched out of the city. They took the road that led toward the setting sun, thinking it was the East, and said among themselves, "See, yonder is the way the kings will ride."

"I have brought a basket of figs," cried one.

"I have dates in a new pañuela," cried another.

"And I," cried a third, "I have brought a sack of sweet limes, they are so cooling."

Thus each in turn showed some small gift that he was bringing for the kings. And while they chatted together one child began to sing the sweet Nativity Hymn. In a moment others joined until the still night air rang with their happy voices.

"Unto us a Child is born,
    Unto us a gift is given.
Hail with holiness the morn,
    Kneel before the Prince of Heaven.

99

Blessed be this day of birth,
God hath given His Son to earth.
Jesu, Jesu, Nene Jesu,
Hallelujah!"

Behind the little hills the sun went down, leaving a million sparks of light upon the road.

"Yonder come the kings!" the children cried. "See the splendor of their shining crowns and how the jewels sparkle on their mantles! They may be angry if they find us out so late; come, let us run home before they see us."

The children turned. Back to the city gates they ran, back to their homes, to the good madres watching for them and their own white beds ready for them.

But one they left behind them on the road: a little, bare-limbed boy whose name was Manuel. He watched until the children had disappeared within the gates, and then he turned again toward the setting sun.

"I have no gift for the kings," he thought, "but there is fresh green grass beside the way that I can gather for the camels."

100

He stopped, pulled his hands full, and stuffed it in the front of the little blue vestido that he wore. He followed the road for a long way until heavy sleep came to his eyes.

"How still it is upon the road! God has blown out His light and soon it will be dark. I wish I were with the others, safe within the city; for the dark is full of fearsome things when one is all alone. . . . Mamita will be coming home soon and bringing supper for Rosita and me. Perhaps to-night there will be an almond dulce or pan de gloria—perhaps. . . . I wonder will Rosita not forget the little prayer I told her to be always saying. My feet hurt with the many stones; the night wind blows cold; I am weary and my feet stumble with me. . . . Oh, Nene Jesu, listen! I also make the prayer: 'Send the three kings before Manuel is too weary and afraid!'"

A few more steps he took upon the road, and then, as a reed is blown down by the wind, Manuel swayed, unknowingly for a moment, and slowly sank upon the ground, fast asleep.

How long he slept I cannot tell you; but a hand on his shoulder wakened him. Quickly he opened his eyes, wondering, and saw—yes, he saw the three kings! Tall and splendid they looked in the star-light, their mantles shimmering with myriad gems. One stood above Manuel, asking what he did upon the road at that late hour.

Manuel rose to his feet, thrusting his hand inside the shirt for the grass he had gathered.

"It is for the camels, señor; I have no other gift. But you—you ride horses this Christmas Eve!"

"Yes, we ride horses. What is that to you?"

"Pardon, señores, nothing. The three kings can ride horses if they wish; only—we were told you rode on camels from the East."

"What does the child want?" The voice was kind, but it sounded impatient, as though the one who spoke had work waiting to be done and was anxious to be about it.

Manuel heard and felt all this wondering. "What if there is not time for them to come, or gifts enough!" He laid an eager, pleading hand on one king's mantle.

"I can hold the horses if you will come this once. It is a little street and hard to find, señores; I thought

*"How Still It Is upon the Road! God
Has Blown Out His Light and
Soon It Will Be Dark"*

perhaps you would leave a present—just one little present for the children there. You told the Christ-child you would give to every child. Don't you remember? There are many of us who have never had a gift—a Christmas gift."

"Do you know who we are?"

Manuel answered, joyfully: "Oh yes, Excellencias, you are the Three Christmas Kings, riding from Bethlehem. Will you come with me?"

The kings spoke with one accord, "Verily, we will."

One lifted Manuel on his horse; and silently they rode into the city. The Keeper slumbered at the gates; the streets were empty. On, past the houses that were garlanded they went unseen; and on through the great streets until they came to the little street at last. The kings dismounted. They gave their bridles into Manuel's hand, and then, gathering up their precious mantles of silk and rich brocade, they passed down the little street. With eyes that scarce believed what they saw, Manuel watched them go from house to house, saw them stop and feel for the shoes between the gratings, the shoes

103

loaned by Enrique, the cobbler, and saw them fill each one with shining gold pieces.

In the morning Manuel told the story to the children as they went to spend one golden doblon for toys and candy and sugared cakes. And a gift they brought for Doña Josefa, too; a little figure of the Holy Mother with the Christ-child in her arms.

And so the promise made in Bethlehem was made again, and to a little child; and it was kept. For many, many years, long after Manuel was grown and had niños of his own, the kings remembered the little street, and brought their gifts there every Christmas Eve.

There was a long silence after David had finished retelling the story to Barney and Johanna that night. The wind was howling outside and beating the snow in hard cakes against the windows.

"Sure, it's up to some one to keep the heart in those two till spring comes," Johanna said at last. "Think o' coming up here from one o' them sizzling-hot places. Holy St. Patrick!"

104

"Aye, and a sick boy and a woman—the frail kind, I'm thinking, not used to lifting her hand to anything heavy."

Barney got up and peered out.

"Well, if the snow's not over our heads the morrow I can beat my way there and keep their fires going for another day."

David got up and joined Barney, sliding a grateful hand through his.

'That would be bully! You know his mother said if they could only keep the big fire going on the open porch and get him out there again she was sure he'd begin to get better. It's been the cold and the staying indoors that has put him back. Do you think, Barney, do you think— You know I could take my turn at it."

"Sure and ye can, laddy. Wait till the morrow and we'll see what we can do—the two of us."

VII. The Trapper's Tale of the First Birthday

THE snow was still falling steadily next morning and David came down to breakfast with an anxious face.

"Now don't be worrying, laddy," was Barney's reassuring greeting. "It takes a powerful lot o' snow to keep a man housed on these hills when he has something fetching him out."

And Johanna, coming in with her hands full of steaming griddle-cakes, brought more encouragement.

"Sure, it's a storm, but not too fierce for a strong man like Barney to brave for them that's in trouble. And I've a can of good soup, jelly and a fresh-baked loaf of bread and some eggs for ye to fetch with ye."

"Oh!" David dug his two hands down deep in his pockets and smiled ecstatically. "I suppose—it's too bad going for me." He appealed to Barney.

"Aye, it is that! Wait till afternoon. The storm may break by then and ye could get out for a bit.

But there's too much weather afoot for a little lad just now."

So David watched Barney make ready alone. Johanna's things were bundled and strapped on his back that his two arms might be free. Then he made fast his snow-shoes—it was no day for skees—and pulling his fur parka down to cover all but his eyes he started off. He looked like a man of the northland. David watched him out of sight, and then he and Johanna fell to the making of a mammoth Christmas cake. There were nuts to be cracked and fruits to be chopped; all good boy work, as Johanna said, and he was glad to be busy.

At noon Barney returned with great news. He had left the South-Americans comfortable and happy. Alfredo was back on his open porch with a monstrous fire roaring up the outside chimney and wood enough stacked within their reach for them to keep it going for a week. The mother had wept over Johanna's gifts. They had lived for days on canned things and stale bread; and she had blessed them all in what Barney had termed "Spanish lingo."

"Sure, ye needn't be fearing about them longer,

laddy; they've the hearts back in them again, and, what's more, they'll stay there, I'm thinking."

As Barney had prophesied, the snow stopped at noon; and after dinner David set forth on his last quest. Warnings from Johanna and Barney followed him out of the lodge: not to be going far—and to mind well his trail. All of which he promised. It was not so very far to the trapper's and the trail was as plain as the hillside itself.

There was no sign of the locked-out fairy, and David expected none. There was but one path left to take. Why should anyone come to show him the way? Although the trail lay down the hill David's going was very slow. He sank deep at every step and where the drifts were high he had to make long detours, which nearly doubled the distance. When he reached the hut at last he met the trapper at his very door-sill. The pack on his back looked full, and David guessed he had just been down to the village for supplies. He eyed David with a grave concern through the opening in his parka; and David wondered whether the rest of the face would be grave, or kind, or forbidding.

108

"Nicholas Bassaraba has few visitors, but you are welcome."

The voice was gruff but not unkindly, and the trapper pushed open the door of his hut and motioned David inside. They stood stamping the snow from their boots; and then the trapper lifted his hood and David saw that he was not at all like the Grimm picture of Bluebeard. He was dark and swarthy-skinned, to be sure, but he wore no beard—only a small mustache—and his eyebrows were not heavy and sinister-looking and his mouth was almost friendly. If the line of gravity should break into a smile David felt sure it would be a very friendly smile. The trapper proceeded to remove the rest of his outer garments and David did the same. When the operation was over they stood there facing each other solemnly—a very large, foreign-looking man and a small American boy.

"Come! This is a day to sit close to the fire and to smoke, if one is big. If one happens to be small, there is—let me see—I think there is chocolate."

The trapper opened a small cupboard and drew out a tinfoiled package which he tossed over to David; then from his pocket he brought a pipe and a pouch. He held the pipe empty between his teeth, while he rebuilt the fire that was low on the hearth. When the fresh wood began to snap he drew up a chair for each of them, close, and proceeded to fill his pipe.

David gazed curiously about the room. It was large and it seemed to serve as kitchen, dining-room, sleeping and living quarters, all combined. The end where they sat by the open fireplace was for living and sleeping; the two comfortable chairs, the table with a reading-lamp, the small case with books, and the couch plainly told this. At the other end was a cook-stove, the cupboard, water-pails, dish-rack, frying-pans and pots hanging against the wall, and a rough pine table with a straight chair. The walls were covered with skins and guns, cartridge-belts, and knives of all descriptions. Altogether David found it a very interesting place, almost as interesting as the man who lived there. His eyes came back to the trapper, who again was considering him gravely.

"It's a bully good place for a man to live in," was David's enthusiastic comment.

"It is good enough for one who must live a stranger, in a strange land."

For all his rough clothes and his calling, the man spoke more like a scholar than a backwoodsman; David had noticed that the first time he had spoken. He spoke with as educated a tongue as his own father; there was a slight foreign twist to it, that was the only difference.

"Where is your country?"

David asked it simply, not out of idle curiosity, but to place the man at home in his own mind.

"My country? Ah, what used to be my country is a little place, not so big as this one state of yours. It is somewhere near the blue Mediterranean, but it is nearer to Prussia. Bah! What does it matter? Nicholas Bassaraba knows no country now but the woods; no people but those." He pointed to the skins on the walls.

"And you kill them!" The accusation was out before David realized it was even on his tongue.

"Ah, what would you have me do? I must live.

Is that not so? And is it not better to live on the creatures of the woods than on one's fellow-men? I kill only what I need for sustenance; for the rest I hurt not one."

There was a hidden fierceness back of the soft voice and David felt immediately apologetic:

"Excuse me! Of course it's all right. I only thought when you spoke of them as your people, and then pointed to their pelts hung around, it sounded sort of barbaric. Sort of like the Indians showing off their scalps, or the head-hunters showing their skulls."

The trapper smiled, and the smile was friendly.

"Youth is ever quick to accuse and as quick to forgive. I know. It is hard for you to understand how I can make them my friends through the long summer; and then, when winter comes and there is a price on their fur, trap them and kill them. But Nicholas Bassaraba kills only enough to bring him in the bare needs of life, and then only for one half the year. For the rest, I am a guide; I carry the packs for the gentlemen campers; I build their fires; I draw their water."

112

The smile changed to a contemptuous curl of the lips. "Such it is to be a man locked out of his own country."

David watched him uncomfortably for an instant. Then he laughed—he could not help it.

"You're not the only one. There are two more of us; and I don't know but what you'd call the flagman another, and Uncle Joab, and maybe the South-Americans, too. You see, I'm just sort of locked out, but the others are truly locked out." And David launched into an account of himself and of what he knew of the others, all but the fairy.

"And is that all? I thought you said there was another person," reminded the trapper.

David blushed consciously. Not that there was the slightest reason for blushing. He certainly felt no shame in his acquaintanceship with the locked-out fairy. It was rather the feeling of shyness in having to put it all into words, and there was always the uncertainty of how a stranger would take it. You never could tell how people were going to take fairies, anyhow. Besides, maybe there were no fairies in what had been this man's country.

113

"The other is not exactly a person," David began, slowly, "not exactly. Say, did you ever see a fairy?"

A look of amazement filled the face of the trapper. It seemed to well up from his eyes and burst forth from his mouth.

"You mean the little people?" he asked at last. "The nixies and the dwarfs and the kobolds, that live under the earth and play pranks on us unsuspecting mortals?"

David nodded.

"Sort of. Have you ever seen one?"

The trapper shook his head vehemently.

"Well, *I* have!" And without in the least understanding why he was doing it David told the story of the locked-out fairy.

When he had finished, the trapper was smiling again.

"Ah, the poor manikin! And here there are three, five, seven of us, all locked out from our homelands; and here was I, Nicholas Bassaraba, thinking I was the only one to feel the homesickness. Bah! Sometimes a man is a fool!"

He thought a minute.

114

"And you say he wore the squirrel coat—the very one I missed from the shed door where it was drying? And all the time I think it was the African from the lumber camp who takes it."

He laughed aloud and stretched his arms out with a little cry of pleasure.

"Ah, it is good, very good, for one outcast to clothe another. To-night I must put out some bread and honey, as my people used to for the little spirits; the manikin may be hungry."

"Tell me," said David, suddenly, "do your people have any stories—stories of Christmas?"

"Christmas!"

The trapper repeated it—almost as if it were a strange word to him. "Wait a minute—keep very still. I will see can I think back a story of Christmas."

David sat without stirring, almost without breathing, as the trapper puffed silently at his pipe. He puffed the bowl quite empty, then knocking the ashes clean out of his pipe he put it back in his pocket again and looked up at David with the old grave look.

115

"There is a people in our country who are called wanderers; some say they have been wanderers for two thousand years. You call them gipsies or Egyptians; we call them 'Tzigan.' Now, they are vagabonds, for the most part, dirty, thieving rascals, ready to tell a fortune or pick a pocket, as the fancy takes them; but—it was not always so. Some say that they have been cursed because they feared to give shelter to Mary and Joseph and the Child when the King of Judea forced them to flee into Egypt. But the gipsies themselves say that this is not true; and this is the story the Tzigan mothers tell their children on the night of Christmas, as they sit around the fire that is always burning in the heart of a Romany camp."

It was winter—and twelve months since the gipsies had driven their flocks of mountain-sheep over the dark, gloomy Balkans, and had settled in the southlands near to the Ægean. It was twelve months since they had seen a wonderful star appear in the sky and heard the singing of angelic voices afar off.

They had marveled much concerning the star

until a runner had passed them from the South bringing them news that the star had marked the birth of a Child whom the wise men had hailed as "King of Israel" and "Prince of Peace." This had made Herod of Judea both afraid and angry and he had sent soldiers secretly to kill the Child; but in the night they had miraculously disappeared—the Child with Mary and Joseph—and no one knew whither they had gone. Therefore Herod had sent runners all over the lands that bordered the Mediterranean with a message forbidding every one giving food or shelter or warmth to the Child, under penalty of death. For Herod's anger was far-reaching and where his anger fell there fell his sword likewise. Having given his warning, the runner passed on, leaving the gipsies to marvel much over the tale they had heard and the meaning of the star.

Now on that day that marked the end of the twelve months since the star had shone the gipsies said among themselves: "Dost thou think that the star will shine again to-night? If it were true, what the runner said, that when it shone twelve months ago it marked the place where the Child lay it may even mark His hiding-place this night. Then Herod would know where to find Him, and send his soldiers again to slay Him. That would be a cruel thing to happen!"

The air was chill with the winter frost, even there in the southland, close to the Ægean; and the gipsies built high their fire and hung their kettle full of millet, fish, and bitter herbs for their supper. The king lay on his couch of tiger-skins and on his arms were amulets of heavy gold, while rings of gold were on his fingers and in his ears. His tunic was of heavy silk covered with a leopard cloak, and on his feet were shoes of goat-skin trimmed with fur. Now, as they feasted around the fire a voice came to them through the darkness, calling. It was a man's voice, climbing the mountains from the south.

"Ohe! Ohe!" he shouted. And then nearer, "O—he!"

The gipsies were still disputing among themselves whence the voice came when there walked into the circle about the fire a tall, shaggy man, grizzled with age, and a sweet-faced young mother carrying a child.

118

"We are outcasts," said the man, hoarsely. "Ye must know that whosoever succors us will bring Herod's vengeance like a sword about his head. For a year we have wandered homeless and cursed over the world. Only the wild creatures have not feared to share their food and give us shelter in their lairs. But to-night we can go no farther; and we beg the warmth of your fire and food enough to stay us until the morrow."

The king looked at them long before he made reply. He saw the weariness in their eyes and the famine in their cheeks; he saw, as well, the holy light that hung about the child, and he said at last to his men:

"It is the Child of Bethlehem, the one they call the 'Prince of Peace.' As yon man says, who shelters them shelters the wrath of Herod as well. Shall we let them tarry?"

One of their number sprang to his feet, crying: "It is a sin to turn strangers from the fire, a greater sin if they be poor and friendless. And what is a king's wrath to us? I say bid them welcome. What say the rest?"

119

And with one accord the gipsies shouted, "Yea, let them tarry!"

They brought fresh skins and threw them down beside the fire for the man and woman to rest on. They brought them food and wine, and goat's milk for the Child; and when they had seen that all was made comfortable for them they gathered round the Child—these black gipsy men—to touch His small white hands and feel His golden hair. They brought Him a chain of gold to play with and another for His neck and tiny arm.

"See, these shall be Thy gifts, little one," said they, "the gifts for Thy first birthday."

And long after all had fallen asleep the Child lay on His bed of skins beside the blazing fire and watched the light dance on the beads of gold. He laughed and clapped His hands together to see the pretty sight they made; and then a bird called out of the thicket close by.

"Little Child of Bethlehem," it called, "I, too, have a birth gift for Thee. I will sing Thy cradle song this night." And softly, like the tinkling of a silver bell and like clear water running over mossy

120

places, the nightingale sang and sang, filling the air with melodies.

And then another voice called to Him:

"Little Child of Bethlehem, I am only a tree with boughs all bare, for the winter has stolen my green cloak, but I also can give Thee a birth gift. I can give Thee shelter from the biting north wind that blows." And the tree bent low its branches and twined a rooftree and a wall about the Child.

Soon the Child was fast asleep, and while He slept a small brown bird hopped out of the thicket. Cocking his little head, he said:

"What can I be giving the Child of Bethlehem? I could fetch Him a fat worm to eat or catch Him the beetle that crawls on yonder bush, but He would not like that! And I could tell Him a story of the lands of the north, but He is asleep and would not hear." And the brown bird shook its head quite sorrowfully. Then it saw that the wind was bringing the sparks from the fire nearer and nearer to the sleeping Child.

"I know what I can do," said the bird, joyously. "I can catch the hot sparks on my breast, for if one

121

should fall upon the Child it would burn Him grievously."

So the small brown bird spread wide his wings and caught the sparks on his own brown breast. So many fell that the feathers were burned; and burned was the flesh beneath until the breast was no longer brown, but red.

Next morning, when the gipsies awoke, they found Mary and Joseph and the Child gone. For Herod had died, and an angel had come in the night and carried them back to the land of Judea. But the good God blessed those who had cared that night for the Child.

To the nightingale He said: "Your song shall be the sweetest in all the world, for ever and ever; and only you shall sing the long night through."

To the tree He said: "Little fir-tree, never more shall your branches be bare. Winter and summer you and your seedlings shall stay green, ever green."

Last of all He blessed the brown bird: "Faithful little watcher, from this night forth you and your children shall have red breasts, that the world may never forget your gift to the Child of Bethlehem."

122

So the Small Brown Bird Spread Wide
His Wings and Caught the Sparks on
His Own Brown Breast!

The trapper smiled gravely at David.

"And that, my friend, was the robin."

"Yes, I know," said David, simply.

He felt very still and quiet inside, almost as if he had dreamed himself into the Romany camp beside the fire, and seen with his own eyes the coming of the Child. It seemed too real, too close to talk about just then; he even forgot to tell the trapper that he liked it. And then the trapper's next words brought him to his feet.

"You are not knowing, it may be, that the night has fallen and the snow is with it again. Come, I think Nicholas Bassaraba will guide you safely to your hilltop."

One glance through the window told David the truth of the words. It was almost dark outside and snow was very thick in the air.

Silently they put on their garments and fastened their snow-shoes. Then with the command to keep close at his heels, the trapper led the way up the trail.

The first thing of which David was conscious was that his strength was going amazingly fast. It seemed but a moment since he had started, and the trapper was climbing very slowly; yet David began to find it unbelievably hard to pull one foot after the other. Gritting his teeth, he stumbled on a few yards farther. Then he fell, picked himself up, and fell again. The third time the trapper helped him to his feet, and, coming behind him, he put a strong hand at David's back and pushed. They struggled on this way for another ten minutes until David fell again. This time it was the trapper's strength alone which righted him, for David's had entirely gone. He stood looking with dazed eyes into the trapper's, ashamed and wholly spent.

"It is all right. It is nothing to be ashamed of." The trapper's voice seemed to come from very far away. "You have climbed many lengths farther than I expected. Now you shall see how Nicholas Bassaraba can pack a hundred pounds when he is guiding for a friend."

He stooped and lifted David on his back, drawing the boy's arms well over his shoulders, and slipping his own firmly under the boy's feet.

That was the last David knew until he felt the ground under his feet again and blinked stupidly at

124

the light Johanna was holding at the open door of the lodge.

"Laddy, laddy, wherever have ye been?"

He heard the distress in Johanna's voice even through his own numbness, and tried to smile reassuringly.

"Barney's been scouring the hill for ye this half-hour."

"He has been to visit a friend, and the friend has brought him back safely," said the trapper. And without another word he disappeared in the snow and the darkness.

VIII. The Christmas That Was Nearly Lost

IT snowed hard all the next day, so hard that even Barney did not venture out; and David spent his time between the kitchen, where Johanna was frosting the Christmas cake, and the woodshed, where Barney was making the "woodpile look mortal weary."

David's mind was full of the happenings of the days that had passed, and of future plans. Everything had been as fine as a boy could wish, but he did not want it to stop. Here it was two days before Christmas, and he was quite sure there was still a lot to be found. The question was, where should he look for it now that the matter of neighbors had been exhausted?

As for the plans, they were growing every minute; but he had decided to say nothing about them to Johanna and Barney until the next day, when they were full-grown. Of one thing David felt certain: nothing could keep Christmas away this year. And so when Barney began to tease him on one of his trips to the woodshed and say that if this weather lasted he guessed the Christmas present from father would get there about Washington's Birthday and that he guessed it would take a Santa Claus with seven-league boots to make the hilltop this year, David just smiled and looked very wise. Something was going to happen; he knew perfectly well that something was going to happen. And so, when it actually did happen, about half-way between dinner and supper time, he was not nearly as surprised as Johanna and Barney, who in a way might have expected it.

They were all three startled by a banging on the door and a stamping and pounding of feet outside. So loud did it sound in the midst of the silence that David thought there must be at least a dozen men. Great was his astonishment, therefore, when Barney swung open the door and a solitary figure stepped in, muffled in fur to the eyes.

"Burrrrrrrrrrr!" boomed the figure, and then he swept off his cap and made a laughing bow.

"Hello, Johanna! Hello, Barney! You never

thought I would remind you right in the midst of a Christmas blizzard of that promise you made last summer. Come now, did you?"

"Holy St. Patrick!" gasped Johanna.

"Mr. Peter!" ejaculated Barney. "But how in the name of all the saints did ye ever make it in this storm?"

The man laughed again.

"Just the usual nerve of the tenderfoot. I left my painting-kit, bag, and canvases with the station-agent. He has promised to send them up if the storm ever stops. And I made a wager with him—a gallon can of next spring's syrup against a box of cigars—that I'd be here by four o'clock. What's the time?"

He had his things off by this time and was looking at his watch.

"Aha! Ten minutes to the good! If your wires are not down, Barney, I'll call him up. He'll be wanting to get ready to tap that maple-tree."

The next moment they could hear his voice booming at the telephone.

"Yes, siree. Here I am, and not even my breath frozen. No, you needn't be sending out that snowplow after me just yet. Only get my things up here as soon as you can. All right!"

Another instant he was back in the room again, vigorously shaking Johanna's and Barney's hands.

"Yes, here I am, to paint those snow canvases I've been going to do so long, and to dodge Christmas."

Then it was that for the first time he became conscious of David in the window recess.

"Bless my soul! Who's this, Johanna?"

Johanna explained, and David came forward and held out an eager hand. He liked this Mr. Peter tremendously, in spite of his last remark, and he was no end glad he had come.

The man returned David's greeting with equal cordiality, while he screwed up his face into a comical expression of mock disgust.

"And I came up here to dodge Christmas! Say, young man, do you think it's possible for any person to get away from Christmas with a boy around?"

"I hope not," laughed David.

"You don't mean to tell me that Christmas hasn't grown into a very tiresome, shabby affair that we would all escape from if we only had the courage?

129

You don't believe there is anything in it nowadays, do you, except the beastly grind of paying your friends back and thanking your lucky stars it doesn't happen oftener than once a year?"

"I certainly do, sir." David spoke as one with authority.

The man rubbed his hands together thoughtfully and his eyes twinkled.

"I see. Johanna and Barney have gone off to fix a bed for me somewhere, so suppose we discuss this matter thoroughly. I'll tell you my personal feelings and you can tell me yours. In the end, maybe we'll compromise!"

He led the way to the window-seat and spread himself out comfortably in one corner; David curled up in the one opposite.

"To begin with," and the man pounded his knee emphatically, "Christmas is responsible for a very bad economic condition. Every one spends more money than he has; that's very bad. Next, you generally put your money into articles that are neither useful nor beautiful; you give your maiden aunt handkerchiefs and she has ten dozen of them already

130

put by in her closet, while you send a box of candy
to the janitor's little girl, who can't go out because
she hasn't any shoes to wear. Now if I could borrow
an invisible cloak and go around a week before
Christmas, peeping in on all the folks that need
things and finding out just what they need, and then
come back on Christmas Eve and drop the gifts unseen beside their doors—well, that might make
Christmas seem a little less shabby. But as it is, I'm
not going to give away an inch of foolish Christmas
this year. And I'm not going to say 'Merry Christmas' to a solitary soul."

"Maybe you'll forget," laughed David. "Now,
is it my turn?"

Mr. Peter nodded.

"Well, I've found out, just lately, that Christmas
isn't things—it's thoughts. And I've an idea how to
make a bully Christmas this year out of nothing."

He hunched up one knee and clasped his arms
about it.

"You see, I used to think that you couldn't have
Christmas without all the store fixings and lots of
presents, just as you do. And when I first came

'way up here I thought it was just naturally 'good-by, Christmas.' Then something happened."

"Suppose you tell me what. We might make a better compromise if I understood just what did happen."

David considered him thoughtfully. Johanna had said while he was out at the telephone that Mr. Peter was a painter, a bachelor chap with no one in particular belonging to him, and David wondered if he would really understand. As Johanna had often said, "There are some things you just can't put through a body's head."

"Things happen 'way up here in the hills that would never happen in the city, never in a hundred years," he began, slowly; and then, gaining courage from the painter's nod of comprehension, he told all about everything. Of course he could not tell all the stories as they had been told to him—there was not time—but he told about them, and particularly about the "heathen."

"And that isn't all," he finished, breathlessly. "I've a great plan for to-morrow night, if Johanna and Barney and you will help."

"We might make that the compromise," smiled Mr. Peter. "What is it?"

David told, and when he had quite finished, the man beside him nodded his head as if he approved.

"What does Johanna say?" he asked.

"I haven't told her yet."

"Well, we'll ask Johanna and Barney to-night. Now let's hunt them up and find out when supper is going to be ready. I'm as hungry as a bear."

But before the plans were unfolded to Barney and Johanna that evening Mr. Peter told a story. He offered it himself as something he had picked up once upon a time, he could not remember just where. He said it was not the kind of a story he would ever make up in the wide world, but he thought it just the kind David might make up.

And here it is as the painter told it two nights before Christmas:

It was four o'clock on Christmas morning and Santa Claus was finishing his rounds just as the milkman was beginning his. Santa had been over to Holland and back again where he had filled

133

millions of little Dutch shoes that stood outside of windows and doors; he had climbed millions of chimneys and filled millions of American stockings, not to mention the billions and trillions of Christmas trees that he had trimmed and the nurseries he had visited with toys too large for stockings. And now, just as the clock struck four, he had filled his last stocking and was crawling out of the last chimney onto the roof where the eight reindeer were pawing the snow and wagging their stumps of tails, eager to be off.

Santa Claus heaved a sigh of relief as he shook the creases out of the great magic bag that was always large enough to hold all the toys that were put into it. The bag was quite empty now, not even a gum-drop or a penny whistle was left; and Santa heaved another sigh as he tucked it under the seat of his sleigh and clambered wearily in.

"By the two horns on yonder pale-looking moon," quoth he, "I'm a worn-out old saint and I am glad Christmas is over. Why, I passed my prime some thousand years ago and any other saint would have

134

taken to his niche in heaven long before this." And he heaved a third sigh.

As he took up the reins and whistled to his team he looked anything but the jolly old saint he was supposed to be; and if you had searched him from top to toe, inside and out, you couldn't have found a chuckle or a laugh anywhere about him.

Away went the eight reindeer through the air, higher and higher, till houses looked like match-boxes and lakes like bowls of water; and it took them just ten minutes and ten seconds to carry Santa safely home to the North Pole. Most generally he sings a rollicking song on his homeward journey, a song about boys and toys and drums and plums, just to show how happy he is. But this year he spent the whole time grumbling all the grumbly thoughts he could think of.

"It's a pretty state of affairs when a man can't have a vacation in nearly five hundred years. Christmas every three hundred and sixty-five days and have to work three hundred and sixty-four of them to get things ready. What's more, every year the work grows harder. Have to keep up with all

135

the scientific inventions and all the new discoveries. Who'd have thought a hundred years ago that I should have to be building toy aeroplanes and electric motors? And the girls want dolls' houses with lights and running water! I declare I'm fairly sick of the sight of a sled or a top, and dolls and drums make me shiver. I'd like to do nothing for a whole year, I tell you—nothing! It's a pretty how d' y' do if the world can't get along for one year without a Christmas. What's to prevent my taking a vacation like any other man? Who's to prevent me?"

The reindeer had stopped outside of Santa's own home and he threw the reins down with a jerk while he tried his best to look very gruff and surly.

"Suppose I try it. By the Aurora Borealis, I *will* try it!"

And then and there Santa Claus began his vacation.

He closed up his workshop, locked the door, and hung the key in the attic. He turned his reindeer loose and told them to go south where they could get fresh grass, for he would not need them for a year and a day. Then he made himself comfortable

136

beside his fire, and brought out all the books and the papers he had been wanting to read for the last fifty years or more, and settled down to enjoy himself. He never gave one thought to the world or what it would do without him; therefore, it never occurred to him to wonder if the news would get in the papers. But you know and I know that in time everything that happens gets into the papers; so the news spread at last all over the world that Santa Claus was taking a vacation and that there would be no Christmas next year. And what do you think happened then?

First of all the Christmas trees stopped growing. "What's the use?" they whispered one to another. "We sha'n't be wanted this year, so we needn't work to put out new shoots or keep especially green and smart-looking." And the holly and the mistletoe heard them, and they said: "Well, why should we bother, either, to get our berries ready as long as we shall not be needed for decoration? Making berries takes a lot of time, and we might just as well spend it gossiping."

Next, the storekeepers began to grumble, and each said to himself, "Well, if Christmas isn't coming

137

this year why should I spend my time making my shop-windows gay with gifts and pretty things?" And the pastry cooks and the confectioners said they certainly would not bother making plum-puddings, Christmas pies, or candy canes.

Soon the children heard about it. For a long while they would not believe it, not until Christmas-time came round again. But when they saw the Christmas trees looking so short and shabby, and the Christmas greens without their berries, and the streets quiet and dull, and the shop-windows without the pretty things in them, they grew sober and quiet, too. And in less time than I can tell you the whole world grew stuffy and stupid and silent and un-lovely. Yes, the whole world!

Now, in a very small house in a very small town that stands just midway between the North Pole and the equator and half-way between the Atlantic and Pacific oceans (you can find the town for yourself on any map if you look for it with these directions) there lived a small boy. He was sturdy and strong, and he had learned two great lessons—never to be afraid and never to give up. He saw what was hap-

138

pening all over the world, because everybody believed that Christmas had been lost, and he said one
day to his mother:

"Mother, little mother, I've been thinking this
long while if Santa Claus could see how things are
going with every one down here he would bring
Christmas back, after all. Let me go and tell him?"

"Boy, little boy," said his mother, "tell me first
how you will find your way there. Remember there
are no sign-posts along the road that leads to Santa
Claus."

But the boy squared his shoulders and took a firm
grip of his pockets and said he, "Why, that's easy!
I'll ask the way and keep on till I get there."

In the end his mother let him go. As he walked
along slowly he questioned everything he passed—
birds, grass, winds, rain, rivers, trees. All these he
asked the fastest road to Santa Claus; and each in
turn showed him the way as far as he knew it. The
birds flew northward, singing for him to follow
after; the grass swayed and bent and made a beaten
path for him; the river carried him safely along its
banks in the tiniest shell of a boat, while the winds

139

blew it to make it go faster. Each horse or donkey that he met carried him as far as he could; and every house door was opened wide to him, and the children shared with him their bowls of bread-and-milk or soup. And wherever he passed, both the children and the grown-ups alike called after him, "You'll tell him; you'll make Santa Claus come and bring our Christmas back to us!"

I cannot begin to tell you the wonderful things that happened to the boy. He traveled quickly and safely, for all that it was a long road with no sign-posts marking the way; and just three days before Christmas he reached the North Pole and knocked at Santa Claus's front door. It was opened by Santa himself, who rubbed his eyes with wonder.

"Bless my red jacket and my fur boots!" he cried in astonishment. "If it isn't a real, live boy! How did you get here, sirrah?"

The boy told him everything in just two sentences; and when he had finished he begged Santa to change his mind and keep Christmas for the children.

"Can't do it. Don't want to. Couldn't if I did. Not a thing made. Nothing to make anything of.

And you can't have Christmas without toys and sweets. Go look in that window and see for yourself." And the old saint finished quite out of breath.

The boy went over to the window Santa had pointed out and, standing on tiptoe, peered in. There was the workshop as empty as a barn in the spring. Spiders had built their webs across the corners and mice scampered over the floors, and that was all. The boy went slowly back to Santa and his face looked very sad.

"Listen to this," he said, and he took a sea-shell from his pocket and held it close to old Santa's ear. "Can you hear anything?"

Santa listened with his forehead all puckered up and a finger against his nose.

"Humph! It sounds like somebody crying away off."

"It's the children," said the little boy, "as I heard them while I passed along the road that brought me here. And do you know why they were crying? Because there are no trees to light, no candles to burn, no stockings to hang, no carols to sing, no holly to make into wreaths—no gladness anywhere.

141

And they are very frightened because Christmas has been lost."

Then Santa did the funniest thing. He blew his nose so hard that he blew tears into his eyes and down his cheeks.

"Fee, fi, fo, fum—I'm a stupid old fool!" said he. "It's too late to do Christmas alone this year; but I might—yes, I might—get help. The world is full of spirits who love the children as much as I do. If they will lend me a hand, this once, we might do it."

Then he went into his house and brought out his wonderful magic whistle that calls the reindeer; and he blew it once, twice, three times; and the next instant the eight were bounding over the snow toward him.

"Go!" he commanded. "Go as quickly as ever you can to all the spirits of the earth, water, and air, and tell them Santa Claus needs their help this year to bring back Christmas to the children."

Away flew the reindeer, and in less time than it takes a cloud to scud across the sky they were back again and with them the most wonderful gathering that has ever been seen since the world was made.

142

There were giants from Norway and trolls from Sweden; there were dwarfs and elves from the mines of Cornwall and fairies from the hills of Ireland; there were brownies from Scotland and goblins from Germany; the Yule nisse and the skrattle from Denmark; and fairy godmothers from everywhere. And from the ocean came the mermaids and the mermen; and from the rivers and brooks came nixies and nymphs and swan maidens. And they all came eager to help. Santa Claus brought down from the attic the key of the workshop and soon everybody was busy at his own particular craft. Not a word was spoken, and for those three days not a soul rested or slept.

The dwarfs and the elves made hammers and planes and saws, knives and slates, trumpets and drums, rings and pins and necklaces of precious stones, for they are the oldest metal-workers under the sun. And the fairies are the finest spinners; and they spun cloth of silk, ribbons and fine laces, yes, and flaxen hair for dolls. The leprechaun, who is the fairy cobbler, made slippers of all colors and sizes from baby-dolls' shoes to real little girls' party slippers and boys' skating-boots. The giants cut down trees and sawed them into logs and boards while the trolls made them into boats and houses, sleds and beds and carriages. The mermaids gathered shells and pearls for beads; the brownies stitched and sewed and dressed the dolls that Santa himself had made. I don't know what the nixies made, unless it was the sea-foam candy.

There was one little goblin too little to know how to do anything, and as no one had time to teach him he wandered about, very unhappy, until a bright idea popped into his head. Then away he scuttled down to the timber-lands to tell the Christmas trees to hurry up and try to grow a bit, because the children would need them, after all.

Well, the long and short of it was that on Christmas Eve everything was finished; and never since Santa Claus was a lad himself had there been such an array of toys. They were so fine and they shone so bright that the children going to bed that night said to one another, "Look up yonder and see the Northern Lights!"

The toys were at last packed in the sleigh and the

boy climbed in on the seat next to Santa, and they were just driving away when a wee old Irish fairy woman stepped up with a great bundle.

" 'Tis stockings," said she. "I've knitted one for every child, for I knew well the poor things would never be hanging up their own this night."

So it happened that the Christmas that was nearly lost was found, after all, and when the children woke up in the morning they saw their stockings full of toys and the tall green trees all trimmed and waiting for them. And when Santa reached the North Pole again, very tired and sleepy, but not at all grumbly, he heard a noise that sounded like running brooks and singing birds and waving grasses and blowing winds all wrapped up together; and he said to himself:

"Dear, dear me! what can that be? It sounds very like the laughter of little children all over the world."

And that is precisely what it was.

When he had finished, Mr. Peter leaned over and whispered to David; and David cleared his throat as if he were going to make a long speech. Then he told his plan to Barney and Johanna and asked them would they do it.

"The heathens!" was all Johanna said; but she sounded distinctly surprised, almost shocked.

"Why not?" said Barney. "Mind, your calling them that doesn't make them it. And what if they were? Is that any reason?"

"Maybe not," agreed Johanna. "Only when a body's got the habit o' thinking folks are not her kind o' folks it takes a powerful bit o' thinking to think them different."

"Sure it does. We'll leave ye to do the thinking while the three of us go out to the woodshed and knock together them sign-posts the little lad is wishing for."

And Barney led the way, while a very happy boy and a man with an amused twinkle in his eyes followed at his heels.

IX. St. Bridget

THE day before Christmas broke cold and clear; and almost before the sun had crested the hill three fur-clad figures were abroad. Two were large and one was small; each carried a post across his shoulders, while the foremost swung an ax in his free hand. They first took the trail for the trapper's, and a dozen yards from the hut they planted one post, knocking it firmly into the snow with the flat of the ax. There it stood straight as could be and about the height of a little lad, with its white sign pointing up the trail they had come and its bands of Christmas green and red—painted by Mr. Peter at the top—warranted to attract attention.

David cast a backward glance of admiration upon it as they turned to cross-cut the ravine and climb the foot-hill that led to the South-Americans' cottage. Yes, it certainly did look fine! And how well the black letters stood out against the white background! With a heart almost bursting with the fullness of contentment David read the sign for the hundredth time:

THIS WAY TO CHRISTMAS

Six o'Clock To-night. Please Come.

David

And the hand pointed straight to the hilltop and the lodge. Another sign was planted by the cottage, and a third by the lumber camp. Then the trio climbed the hill again. At the lodge Barney picked up a fourth post. He was going down to the village for some necessary supplies and he had been appointed to leave the sign for the flagman.

"There's just one thing that's the matter," said David, as he and Mr. Peter started out with knives and bags to hunt for ground-pine and other Christmas greens. "It's the South-Americans. I don't see how they could possibly get here. Why, the sick boy has hardly enough strength to walk across the room. And you couldn't expect a lady to climb a mountain on snow-shoes, just for Christmas."

Mr. Peter laughed.

148

"You can never tell what's going to happen Christmas Eve. Maybe the fairy will loan them his wishing-cap. Or Santa, himself, may swing round here on his way to the city and bring them along. I wouldn't begin to worry about who's not coming until it's too late for them to get here."

All through that crisp winter morning David and Mr. Peter plowed back and forth between the woods and the lodge, carrying green of every description, with intervals spent beside the kitchen stove, warming up. And early in the afternoon they started decorating the hall and living-room, while Johanna and Barney concentrated their efforts in the kitchen. Barney had succeeded in rooting out untold treasures from the shelves of the "variety store" in the village; and he had brought home several cans of silver paint and rolls of red tissue-paper, besides some white and red candles.

With these Mr. Peter and David created miracles. They silvered bunches of the pine-cones and hung them on their drooping green branches above the doorways and windows. They trailed the ground-pine across the ceiling from corner to corner, and

149

about the mantel, hanging from it innumerable tiny red bells fashioned from the red paper. They stood two tall young spruces on either side of the window niche and these they trimmed with strips of popcorn, silvered nuts and pine-cones and red and white candles. And every window had a hemlock wreath made gay with cranberries.

And Barney and Johanna? They were likewise performing miracles. When David and Mr. Peter had finished and given their work a last survey and exchanged a final round of mutual congratulations they went into the kitchen to behold the others' handiwork.

There was the table lengthened out and covered with a snowy-white cloth. In the center, surrounded by a wreath of green, stood the mammoth Christmas cake; and at the four corners stood tall white candles in crystal candle-sticks. At one end was a cold baked ham resplendent with its crust of sugar and cloves and its paper frill of red and white. At the other was a red Japanese bowl filled with the vegetable salad that had made Johanna famous; while dotted all about the table were delectable dishes of

150

all sorts—jams and jellies, nuts, raisins, savory pickles, and a pyramid of maple-sugar cream. But it was from the stove that the appetizing odors came: rolls baking, coffee steaming, and chicken frying slowly in the great covered pan.

"It smells too good to be true," cried Mr. Peter, clapping his hands. "Never was there such a Christmas supper! Come, David, boy, we will have to scramble into some festal raiment to do honor to Johanna's cooking, although I am not quite sure that I have anything to dress up in but a pair of gold sleeve-links and a red necktie."

"Ye might be making a prayer while ye're dressing that somebody will come to help eat it up. I've said to Barney a score o' times since dinner that there's just as much likelihood that not a mortal soul will show his face here this night."

"Why, Johanna!" David protested.

"I know, laddy. But mind, ye've not seen one of them but once, yourself, and I'm a stranger to them. Never matter; only if no one comes ye'll all be eating ham and fried chicken for the rest o' the year." And Johanna ended with a good-humored laugh.

151

Before six they were gathered in the living-room with the candles lighted and the fire blazing uproariously on the hearth.

"It's all so fine and like mother used to have. I believe I shall be wishing somebody 'Merry Christmas' before I know it," shouted Mr. Peter. Then he held up a warning finger. "Hush! What's that?"

They all listened. There was certainly a noise outside; it sounded as if some one was feeling for the knob. David was away like a flash to the hall and had flung open the door wide. The next moment his voice came back to the others, ringing with gladness:

"Uncle Joab! Oh, Uncle Joab! This is just bully!"

The bent figure of the old darky stumbled in out of the night. He carried two bundles under his arm, each wrapped in layers of gunny-sack; and he blinked, open-mouthed, at the lights and the faces that gathered about him.

"It sure is a befo'-de-war Chris'mus!" he ejaculated. Then he sniffed the air like an old dog on a scent. " 'Pon ma soul, dat's fried chick'n or Uncle Joab's no sinner!"

They all laughed; and one by one they shook Uncle Joab's hand as David introduced them. Once divested of his outside things, the old man turned his attention to his bundles and unwrapped them with great care. The first turned out to be his fiddle and he patted it lovingly.

"When I fust cotch sight o' dat yeah post dis mo'nin' I wa'n't sure dat de sign was meant fo' no ole nigger like Uncle Joab. Den I look 'round, but dere doan't 'pear to be nobody else. So I brings along de ole fiddle, 'ca'se I reckon dat dey'll be glad to see him if dey 'ain't got no welcome fer me."

"Sure, we're hearty glad to see the both o' ye." And Barney spoke out for them all.

The old man beamed his gratitude as he unwrapped his second bundle. It held a paper sack; and Uncle Joab viewed the contents with approval before he handed it to David.

"M'lasses corn-balls; Chris'mus gif' fo' li'l' boy," he chuckled.

David's thanks were cut short by the stamping

of feet outside and a clang of the knocker. Again he flew to the door and found the eyes of the trapper looking down upon him with grave pleasure.

"Nicholas Bassaraba, my friend," he said, proudly, and this was the way he made the trapper known to the others.

The flagman came next, the icicles hanging to his scrubby mustache, his little blue eyes dancing with anticipation. He was quite out of breath and it was some minutes before he could respond properly to his warm welcome.

"Zo, Fritz Grossman has some friends this Chreestmas; eet es goot!" And his eyes danced harder than ever. He felt down in the pockets of his greatcoat and brought out his hands full of red apples. Their glossy skins bespoke much careful polishing. "Chreestmas apples for the knabelein. He remembers the tale? Ja!"

The stillness outside was suddenly broken by the jingle of bells—sleigh-bells coming nearer and nearer. This time it was Mr. Peter who reached the door first; he had taken down the hall lantern and was holding it high above his head as he peered out.

"Whoa, there!" came a voice from the dark. "That you, Mr. Peter? I ca'late I wouldn't ha' broken through no road like this for no one else. But here we be, all hunky-dory!"

"Well, I ca'late there isn't another man who could have done it. You bring in the lad and I'll see to the lady." And Mr. Peter went out into the darkness, lantern in hand.

The next moment David knew his cup of happiness had filled to the brim; for in strode the village stage-driver with Alfredo in his arms, while behind them came Mr. Peter supporting the mother.

"It's splendid! It's perfectly splendid!" David said over and over again, as he helped to unbundle the South-Americans and make the sick boy comfortable in the great lounging-chair by the fire.

"It is wonderful," said the mother, softly. "To have the aloneness and heart-hunger and then to find the friend!" And her arm slipped about David's shoulders in a way his own mother had.

"Supper's ready," called Johanna from the kitchen. "And, Barney, suppose ye and Mr. Peter fetch out the lad, just as he is in his big chair."

155

They put Alfredo at one end of the table, while Johanna sat at the other behind the great, steaming coffee-pot. Uncle Joab insisted on serving every one, bustling back and forth from the stove to the kitchen, his black face radiating his pleasure.

"Lordy gracious!" he would burst forth every few minutes. "Dis yeah nigger hasn't served a supper like dis not since he was back in ole Virginy. Jes' smell dat fried chicken! Humm!" And they could not persuade him to take his place among them until every one else's plate was full.

What a supper it was! The men who had been shifting for themselves alone in their cabins or huts, the South-Americans who had been living on food put up in cans and tins, were quite sure they had never tasted such a Christmas feast. And every one had stories to tell, memories of his own homeland which brought a flush to his cheeks and a sparkling moisture to his eyes. Only David was silent, his ears too full of what he was hearing, his heart too full of what he was feeling, yes, and maybe his mouth too full of Christmas cheer for him to talk.

It was not until the last crumb of the Christmas

cake had been eaten and the last drop of coffee been drained by Uncle Joab and they had gathered about the fire once more, that David spoke.

"First, let's have Uncle Joab play some of his jigs and sing with his fiddle just as I heard him that day at the camp. Then let's have Johanna tell us a story. She's the only one who hasn't told a Christmas story."

So of course David had his wish. Uncle Joab tuned up and played all the rollicking airs he knew, following them with the old plantation songs so dear to the hearts of even those who have only sojourned in the South. And when he was tired and insisted that "de ole fiddle must rest" Johanna drew her chair closer to the hearth and began the story of St. Bridget.

In Ireland St. Bridget is sometimes called "St. Bridhe of the Mantle," and that is because the people of the hills would not be forgetting the way she came to be at Bethlehem when Our Lord was born, or the rest of the miracle.

It was to the little island of Iona that she came

157

when she was naught but a child, and her coming there was strange. Her father was Doughall Donn, a prince of Ireland; but because of a sin, which he swore was not his, he was banished from his Green Isle. He took the child and left at night in a small boat; and the winds blew and the waves carried them toward Alba. But when they were still a long way off the winds blew into a storm and the waves reared themselves into a tempest and the boat was dashed upon the rocks. It was the dawn of that day that Cathal, the arch-druid of Iona, looked down from his holy hill where he had been lighting the sacrificial fire to the Sun God, for in those days it was before the Lord had walked the earth; and he saw below him on the beach the figure of a man washed up by the storm and lying as if dead. He hurried to the place and found not only the man, but a wee girl child, and she beside him, playing with the shells and digging her pink toes into the wet sand. The man was not dead, only stupid with the sea-water; and Cathal brought them both to a herdsman's hut and saw that they were fed and cared for.

That night he had a strange vision concerning the

158

child; he dreamed that spirits from heaven descended to watch over her while she slept; and when he was for knowing why they should guard her with celestial care they made this answer:

"Know ye, she is holy and blest above all maidens. For some day it shall come to pass that she shall cradle the King of Love upon her breast and guard the Lord of Creation while He sleeps."

And when the vision broke it was Cathal himself that came and watched beside the herdsman's hut where the child slept. So Doughall Donn was made welcome in Iona for the sake of the child; and the druids gave him a hut and herd of his own and saw to it that neither he nor the child should want for anything.

It was midsummer and the day of Bridget's birth, marking the twenty-first year; and at ring o' day while the dew still clung to the grass Bridget left her father's hut and climbed the holy hill. Of all the dwellers on Iona she alone was let watch the lighting of the sacrificial fire and she alone was let hear the chanting of the druid's hymn to the Sun God. This day she was clad in white with a wreath of the rowan berries on her hair and a girdle of them about her waist; and she looked fair as the flowers of the dawn.

As she climbed the hill the wild creatures came running to her for a caress and the birds hovered above her head or perched on her shoulder. She listened to the chanting of the hymn; she bided till the flames of the fire met and mingled with the shafts of the sun. Then a white bird called from the thicket and she followed. She followed him over the crest of the hill; and behold! when she came out to the other slope, 'twas another country she was seeing!

Here were no longer the green fields and the pastures filled with sheep, or the sea lying beyond. It was a country of sand and hot sun; and the trees and the houses about her were strange. She found herself standing by a well with a strangely fashioned jug in her hand, and her father beside her.

"Bridhe," said he, "ye are a strange lass. Are ye not knowing that the well has not held a drop of water for a fortnight, and did ye think to fill your pitcher now?"

She smiled faintly.

"I was not remembering."

160

Her father drew her away toward the village that lay beneath them, the village of Bethlehem.

"Bridhe," said he again, "the drouth has been upon us these many months. The wells are empty, even the wine is failing, and the creatures are dying on our hands. I shall leave the inn this night in your care while I take the camels and the water-skins and ride for succor. There is a well, they tell me, in a place they call the Mount of Olives which is never dry; and 'tis a three days' journey or more there and back."

"And what is it that I should be doing, with ye away?" asked Bridget.

They had reached the door of the inn by now, and Doughall Donn opened it for her to pass through.

"Ye are to stay here, birdeen, and keep the door barred against my return. Not a soul is to pass over the threshold while I am gone. Ye are not to open to the knock of man, woman, or child—mind that!"

"But, father, what if some one should come in mortal need—famished with the hunger or faint with the thirst?"

He led her to the rude cupboard and pointed to the nearly empty shelves.

"There is a cruiskeen of ale and a cup o' water, a handful o' dry dates and some oaten cake; that is all of food or drink left in the inn. 'Twill no more than last ye till I return, and if ye fed another ye would starve. So mind the promise I put on ye this night. Ye are to shelter no one in the inn while I am gone."

Bridget watched her father drive the camels out of the courtyard; she barred the door on his going and for two days no foot crossed the threshold of the inn. But on the night of the third day, as Bridget was making ready for bed, she heard the sound of knocking on the door.

"Who is it and what is it ye are wanting this night?" called Bridget from within, keeping the door fast.

"God's blessing on this house!" came in a man's voice out of the dark. "I am Joseph, a carpenter of Arimathea, and this is Mary who is after needing a woman's help this night. She is spent and can go no farther. Will ye give us shelter?"

162

"That I cannot. The promise is laid on me to give neither food nor shelter to living soul till my father comes hither. Were it not for that 'tis a glad welcome I'd be giving the both of ye."

And then a woman's voice came out of the darkness, a voice that set her breasts to be trembling and her heart to be leaping with joy.

"Are ye forgetting me, Bridhe astore?" said the voice.

Bridget opened the grating in the door and looked out. There she saw a great-shouldered giant of a man, covered with beard, and beside him was a wee gray donkey, and on the donkey rode a woman, who turned her face to Bridget and smiled. And the wonder of that smile drew Bridget's hand to the latch.

She opened the door wide and bade them enter. She laid before them what ale and dates and oaten cake was left, and watched them eat in silence.

Then she beckoned them to the courtyard.

"Yonder is the byre clean with fresh straw; and the creatures are gentle. Half the promise have I

163

broken this night; I have given ye food. But shelter ye must take outside the inn. Come!"

She led the way to the byre and left them there, hurrying back to bar the door of the inn again. But as she was fastening the latch she heard the sound of much travel abroad, and looking out she saw it was her father's camels returning. There was great gladness in her welcome—aye, and there was sadness for the breaking of the promise.

"See," said she, drawing her father in. "I gave them food—only food. They are resting in the byre." But when she went to gather up the dish that had been empty, behold it was filled with dates and oaken cake! And the cruiskeen was filled with ale!

" 'Tis a miracle!" said Bridget, the breath leaving her; and even as she spoke the strange thing happened.

Outside came the sound of falling rain, not gentle as a passing shower, but the steady beat, beat, beat of the rainy season.

"The drouth is broken," said Doughall Donn, adding, with wonder in his voice: "What manner of folk are those yonder? Are ye not minding the

164

prophecy: 'The King of Love, Ruler of the World and All Time, shall be born on the first night of rain following the great drouth; and He shall be born in a byre outside an inn.' Come, let us see!"

He drew Bridget with him across the courtyard, but before ever they entered the byre they saw the holy light and heard singing that was not of this earth. And when they came inside there was Mary upon the hay, and beside her lay a new-born child.

"Aigh! the blessed wee one!" whispered Bridget, kneeling down beside them. "I am thinking ye had better rest, Mary astore; give me the birdeen to nurse while ye sleep." And with hunger-arms she reached out for the Holy Child and wrapped it in the white mantle that she wore.

"Aye, take Him," said Mary. "I would I might, in the years to come, give my babe to every barren breast. But ye, Bridget, are alone blest."

And through the long night Bridget cradled the Child while Mary slept and the kine looked on, kneeling in their stalls. And when day broke, Bridget closed her eyes and slept, too, for the weariness was upon her.

It was the call of a white bird that wakened her. She started up with a cry of fear and her arms reached over her breast for the Child, but the Child was gone. And when she looked about her she saw she was standing on the crest of the holy hill, while beyond her lay green fields and pastures full of sheep, and her father's hut, and the blue bay of Iona at her feet.

" 'Tis all a dream," she said, the wonder on her. And then she looked at the mantle she wore. It was woven with golden threads into marvelous pictures of birds and beasts and angels. And Bridget went slowly down the holy hill, the mantle about her; and when she came to her father's hut she found she had been gone for a year and six months.

X. The Chapter After the End

THE last thing David remembered that night was hearing Mr. Peter's voice booming out a "Merry Christmas" to each of the departing guests. Incredible and humiliating as it might seem, Johanna had had to help him to bed! He was so worn out with the work and the joy of all that had happened that day that his eyes would not stay open long enough for him to make the proper going-to-bed arrangements for himself.

And the first thing David thought about when he woke Christmas morning was the locked-out fairy. Yes, even before he thought about the gift that was coming that day from father.

Where was the fairy? He had not seen him for two days, had not come upon a single track that might have been his in all his tramping through the woods for greens. He did not like to think it, but perhaps the fairy was shivering and hungry in some hollow tree or deserted rabbit-burrow, homesick and

alone, while he, David, had almost, yes, had almost
unlocked the door that led back into his old world—
almost found opening-time.

It did not seem fair that now the fairy should be
left out, when his own happiness was the fairy's
doing, after all; when he would never have found
the way to Christmas or the way out of loneliness if
the fairy had not made the trail for him to follow.
He made up his mind at once, even before he was
out of bed, that he would spend Christmas day hunting for the fairy and seeing to it that he had all the
comforts that mere mortals could supply.

Then he remembered the Christmas gift that was
coming. Perhaps it was something he could share
with the fairy. He had thought about it a good
many times in the days since father's letter had come;
and he had speculated a good deal as to what it could
be. It might be some strange curiosity from the
East—father was tremendously interested in curi-
osities; or it might be books, as father was fond of
books. Of one thing he was certain, it would be
something that father would like himself; he could
not imagine father choosing anything else.

168

Breakfast was late. They had seen Christmas day in before the last guest had gone the night before; and when there are no stockings to empty, no presents to unwrap, there is no need to hurry breakfast along or speed the day. Everybody was in rare good humor. Mr. Peter swung David to his shoulder and marched three times round the table, singing, "Good King Wencelas."

"Faith, 'tis the best keeping of Christmas I have seen since I came to this country," was Barney's comment.

"I think 'tis the best I ever had," said Johanna.

"I know what I'm going to do," shouted Mr. Peter. "I'm going to steal the chart and take it back with me to the city; and next year when the notion begins to take me that I want to dodge Christmas again I'll unroll the chart, take a good look at it, and make straight for the right road. And I tell you what!" He put two hands on David's shoulders. "I believe it would be just as well to have you along, young man. With you there, and Barney and Johanna, I couldn't go wrong, you know; and we could take a lot of other poor, tired mortals on the

169

road with us and show them such a Christmas as would warm their hearts and keep their memories green for the rest of their lives."

"Aye, that's true," agreed Johanna. "But if ye don't sit down and stop talking, Mr. Peter, ye'll be taking the road to a cold breakfast."

They were not half through when a knocking came at the front door. Barney answered it, and came back in a moment with a puzzled smile on his face.

" 'Tis your friend, the trapper," he said to David. "He'll not come in; but he wants to be speaking with ye, laddy."

Wondering much what it could mean, David slipped from his chair and went into the hall. The trapper was standing just inside the door, and he was holding something small and gray in his great fur mitten.

"Nicholas Bassaraba has brought you something. It was there this morning, hanging on a peg in the woodshed. See!" He held up the coat of a gray squirrel.

"Where— How did it get there?"

170

The trapper shrugged his shoulders.

"Ah—how should I know? But I can guess. And you? Where are your wits, your fancy, my friend?"

David took the skin between his hands, rubbing his fingers through the soft fur.

"You think he brought it back? That he—"

"Is it not possible? He has gone back to his country—his people. He is no longer what you call 'locked out.' So he gives back again what he borrowed from Nicholas Bassaraba—the coat. Ah, he is a fairy of honor; and I bring it to you, my friend. It may be that is what the manikin intends when he hangs it on the peg. At any rate, it is yours to keep always; a symbol, a memory of how you found the way to the cabins and the hearts of some lonely men. Yes, this you shall keep; while we keep other memories. It is well."

He turned toward the door to be gone, but David held him back.

"But it isn't just memories, you know. I'm coming back again and again to hear more stories of the gipsies. And in the spring, Barney says, perhaps

171

you'll help me find a den of young foxes or raccoons. I've always wanted to have some to tame."

The trapper smiled.

"Even so. We will go together. It is not hard to find the litters of young things in the spring; they are very plentiful."

After the trapper had gone David stood a minute thinking before he went back to his breakfast. So this was a white winter. And Johanna had said that about as often as a white winter the fairy raths opened on Christmas Eve—just for that night. Somehow the fairy must have known this would happen; and he had gone back to Ireland, back to his rath, a locked-out fairy no longer.

There was a broad smile of happiness on David's face as he took his seat at the table again.

"Ye certainly look pleased with your present," teased Barney. "What did he bring ye now—just a squirrel's skin?"

"No, not just! Wait until to-night and I'll tell you and Johanna one of your own Irish stories. Only this one will have American improvements."

172

And David nodded his head mysteriously after Johanna's own fashion.

It was then that the telephone rang and Barney answered it. If there had been a puzzled smile on his face before, when the trapper came, there was a veritable labyrinth of expressions now as he came back to the kitchen. There was a tangle of mystery, astonishment, delight, incredulity, and excitement; and even Johanna herself could not guess what lay at the heart of it all.

"Speak up, Barney, man," she cried. "What has happened ye?"

And Mr. Peter slapped him on the back and thundered at him: "Wake up, sir! You look as if you'd been dreaming about fairies!"

"Maybe I have," chuckled Barney; then he sobered. "No, 'twas the station-agent that 'phoned. He says the wee lad's Christmas present has come from across the water, and he's sending it up this minute by the stage-driver."

"Is it as large as that?" gasped David in surprise.

"Aye, it's a good size." And Barney chuckled harder than ever.

Johanna looked at him sharply.

"Faith, I'm believing ye know what the wee laddy's getting."

"Maybe I do, but I'm not going to be telling one of ye—not till it gets here."

It was a very excited group that gathered in the window nook and waited for the stage-driver to make the trip up to the hilltop. It would take some time, they knew, for the going was slow, as he had reported the night before, and they all waited with a reasonable amount of patience. All but Barney. He strode up and down the living-room, slapping his knees and chuckling to himself as if he were bursting with the rarest, biggest piece of news a man ever had to keep to himself.

"For the love of St. Patrick, can't ye sit down and keep quiet a minute, man?" Johanna asked in desperation. "By the way ye are acting ye'll have the lad thinking his father's sent him a live elephant or some one o' those creatures that run wild in the East."

With a final triumphant whoop Barney sprang to the door and threw it open.

174

" 'Tis almost here!" he cried. "I can hear the bells on the sleigh."

"So can I," cried David. "And there's the team and the sleigh and— Why, there's somebody in it besides the driver!"

He was off from the window-seat and beside Barney at the door, and the others followed quickly, as the driver touched the team with his whip and the sleigh flew into plain view. Yes, there certainly was some one on the seat with the driver!

"Mercy on us!" gasped Johanna.

"Merry Christmas!" shouted Barney and Mr. Peter together.

But David could not shout. He could only keep whispering to himself, over and over: "Mother! *It's mother!*"

THE END